"I learned a lot this week. Organic farming is definitely a labor of love. But I also learned a lot about myself, and what I really want out of life." Miles stared deep into Kyla's eyes, as if she were the only one in the gazebo.

Her lips parted, and she gave him a hesitant look before asking, "What's that?"

"A woman who shares my passions and dreams of one day ridding the world of hunger. Someone who's not waiting on the government or anybody else to do what needs to be done in this world. That's what I want."

Miles needed to touch her at that moment. He wanted to taste her lips and wrap her in his arms. Once he walked away from here the moment would be lost. He didn't know if he'd ever see her again, but he wanted to make sure she knew how he felt.

He closed the distance between them and wrapped his arm around her waist. "Thank you for the education." He covered her mouth with his, and closed his eyes while savoring the minty taste of her lips.

Dear Reader,

Thank you so much for purchasing *Something About You*, the third book in the Coleman House series. I hope you enjoyed Rollin's story, *When I Fall in Love*, and his baby sister Corra's story, *The Only One for Me*. In this book, you get to see their cousin, Kyla Coleman, the quiet PhD candidate, blossom into her own. This is the story of how two people from opposing teams find common ground and even a little love during the summer's harvest.

This series came to me while riding through the countryside in Kentucky and seeing a massive house that reminded me of Tara from *Gone with the Wind*. My curiosity about who lived there got the better of me, and I created my own little Southern family. Up next in the series, Tracee Coleman, Kyla's sister, slows down long enough to find love.

Thanks,

Bridget Anderson

Something About You

Bridget Anderson

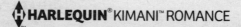

HARLEQUIN® KIMANI™ ROMANCE

Recycling programs
for this product may
not exist in your area.

ISBN-13: 978-1-335-21661-8

Something About You

Printed in U.S.A.

Bridget Anderson writes provocative stories about smart women and the men they love. She has over nine published novels and two novellas to date. Her romantic suspense novel, *Rendezvous*, was adapted into a made-for-television movie.

When Bridget's not writing, she loves to travel. She's fallen in love with Paris, France, and can't wait to get back to Ghana, West Africa. She's a native of Louisville, Kentucky, who currently resides north of metro Atlanta with her husband and a big dog that she swears is part human.

To find out about future release dates, past releases or to sign up for her newsletter, visit her on the web at www.bridgetanderson.net. She loves to connect with readers. You can follow her on Twitter, @Banders319, or at www.Facebook.com/banders319.

Books by Bridget Anderson

Harlequin Kimani Romance

When I Fall in Love
The Only One for Me
Something About You

I'd like to dedicate this one
to my critique partner, Shirley Harrison,
who helped me out of more than a few rough spots.

Chapter 1

The back of the red Ford pickup rattled a bit as it traveled down the Danville, Kentucky dirt road that led to row after row of beautiful bright-red strawberries. Guests of The Coleman House B and B sat on benches on either side of the truck bed with wicker baskets in hand. Kyla Coleman, their tour guide, and the assistant farm manager lived for these morning rides out to the fields. She loved watching the guests get excited about picking organic produce. Educating people about the benefits of organic food was the premise of her PhD thesis and her passion in life.

The truck stopped just short of a row of strawberries.

Kyla stood up, stretching her long legs, and smiled. "Okay, everyone, can I get your attention, please?" She tried not to laugh at two teenage girls sitting at the end of the truck who were trying unsuccessfully to fan away the dust that had kicked up after Kevin, her co-worker brought the truck to a halt.

A couple from Tennessee with their young son, another couple from Michigan who had flown in to attend a niece's wedding, and Ms. Barbara Jean, who checked into the B and B for her birthday every year, all sat attentively, awaiting Kyla's instructions.

"Start on the rows to my left and work your way down the vines. The truck will stay right here should you need another basket." She reached down to pick one up. "I know everything here is organically grown, but we ask that you not eat more strawberries than you put in your basket," she said with a smile.

Several of the guests laughed and nodded.

"I always have my share," Ms. Barbara Jean said, with a chuckle and roll of her eyes.

Kyla grinned at the group, knowing they couldn't wait to pop a juicy red berry into their mouths. "And remember, you're picking enough for strawberry pies for dessert and a few other treats." She moved past everyone and jumped down from the back of the truck. She reached underneath the truck bed and pulled down the steps Kevin had installed to assist guests on and off the truck.

"So, how much time do we have?" someone asked.

Kyla looked down at her watch. "How does forty-five minutes sound?"

"Good, that's plenty of time," a voice responded.

Kyla walked around the side of the truck as the guests headed for the fields, swinging their baskets. Kevin stepped out from behind the driver's seat in the same uniform as Kyla, khakis and a beige polo shirt. He had worked for her cousin Rollin, who owned The Coleman House farm and B and B, for over five years now. Every morning he drove guests of the B and B out into the fields to pick fruits and vegetables that her Aunt Rita, the cook, would later prepare for dinner.

"Beautiful morning, isn't it?" Kevin asked in a chip-
er voice.

Kyla inhaled the sweet country air. "That it is," she agreed before shoving her hands into the back pockets of her khakis and staring off into the vast green fields of the farm. Since she'd joined the farm crew nine months ago on a part-time basis, her favorite job was assisting Kevin with the morning tours. Anything she didn't know about the farm, he could fill in.

"Well, are you ready to present at World Hunger Day?" he asked. "You look cool as a cucumber this morning, but I bet you're nervous as all get-out."

"I am. I was up half the night rehearsing my presentation, but I can't keep the quiver out of my voice."

"You'll do fine," he assured her. "I've never met anyone who knows more about organic farming than you and Rollin."

"Yeah, but not only will there be University of Kentucky faculty members present, but other authorities in the field. And I'll be speaking on a panel with some really smart and educated people, and some of them know far more than I do."

"Bet they're not working on their PhD like you are. Besides, your professor wouldn't have asked you if he didn't think you'd make an excellent speaker."

Kyla laughed. "Thanks Kev. I think I'm the only student of Professor Abraham's who's created a business plan for their non-profit with a long-term plan of action for the organization. That's what he's impressed with."

One of the teenage girls came for another basket. Kevin reached inside the truck and handed it to her, smiling as she walked back to join the others.

"So, how's your girlfriend these days?" Kyla asked.

Kevin looked at her and started laughing. "What? All I did was look. She's cute."

"Uh-huh. Don't get yourself in trouble again."

"Isn't it about time for you to leave for Lexington?

Wouldn't want you to be late. And why did you choose to come out here, anyway? I could have handled the tour myself this morning."

"I don't have to be there until after noon, and working kind of settles my nerves. Takes the edge off." She shook her hands out, and took a deep breath.

After the strawberry fields came the vegetable gardens, followed by a brief farm tour before the guests were carried back to the B and B. As the truck turned in, Kyla noticed something she didn't usually see at the Coleman Farm—her older brother Gavin's truck. Gavin worked with their father on their small farm in Nicholasville. At nine in the morning he should be miles away, busy at work. So why was he here? She hadn't seen her parents in almost a month, since she moved out of student housing and into the B and B for the summer, so she hoped everything was okay. As she climbed off the truck, she cursed herself for not going home more often.

She hurried through her goodbyes to the guests before going inside and walking to the back of the house where the family quarters were located. The house staff was finishing up breakfast, but she didn't see Gavin anywhere. Corra, Rollin's sister, walked into the kitchen.

"Morning, Kyla, how was the tour this morning?" Corra asked as she poured herself a cup of coffee.

"Great, as usual. Lots of questions." Corra and her two kids were Kyla's favorite cousins. When she had the time, she helped Corra in the gift shop and just loved being in her company. She was funny, and she never asked nosy questions, trying to pry into Kyla's personal business like some other family members.

Rita Coleman, Kyla's aunt by marriage, came whirling through the kitchen. "Kyla, honey, grab yourself something to eat. You don't want to sit down in front of them folks with your stomach growling."

"I'm fine. I ate something this morning." Rita was the backbone of The Coleman House. After her cousin's parents were killed in a car crash, Rita had stepped up as a surrogate mother and later joined the staff of the B and B. They couldn't run the house without her. She cooked all the meals, tended a beautiful garden out back and did a little housekeeping, all before going home to her husband at night. It was her personal touches that helped distinguish their B and B from others in town.

"Oh, that's right. It's World Hunger Day, isn't it?" Corra asked. "Kyla, aren't you supposed to be at the University of Kentucky this morning?"

"I don't have to be there for a little while. I saw Gavin's truck out front. Is he here?"

Rita set a plate in front of Corra and instructed her to fill it up. "He's out back with Rollin. Sure was glad to see him this morning. Gavin and your daddy are so busy these days, we hardly get to see them."

"I know. I haven't seen him myself in a while. I hope everything's okay at home."

"I'm sure it's just fine. But why don't you run on out and say hello before you go. You know how Gavin is—one never knows when he'll be this way again."

"I think I will." Kyla looked down at her watch. She had a few minutes.

Several yards behind the B and B was a large barn where Rollin kept a lot of the smaller farm equipment. Kyla spotted both men standing just outside the barn as she crossed the yard. Her younger brother was almost as tall as her cousin Rollin.

After graduating from high school, Gavin had gone straight to work with their father. No amount of prodding and persuasion could talk Gavin into going to college.

He said he'd go to the local community college and take some business classes, but that never happened. Instead, Gavin married a local girl, began having babies and never left the farm. He'd moved his family in with their parents last summer.

Rollin put his hand on Gavin's shoulder and gestured to him as Kyla approached. "Hey, look who it is."

She strolled up to them. "I see, and I'm surprised. What brings you to Danville?" she asked as she greeted her brother with a hug.

Gavin smiled and hugged her back. "I came to catch up with you and Tracee, and then I saw Rollin out here so I thought I'd pick his brain a minute."

Their older sister, Tracee, was also part of the B and B staff. She baked and helped Rita prepare meals in the kitchen. "Well, I don't know where Tracee is, but I've only got a minute. I'm speaking on a panel in Lexington today."

Rollin looked at his watch. "Speaking of which, shouldn't you be there?"

"She's scared," came a loud voice from behind them.

Kyla turned around to see Tracee with her full head of natural curls bouncing as she walked toward them. Her free-flowing mane epitomized why Kyla nicknamed her Good Time Girl. Tracee roamed freely through the world, pursuing things that made her happy. She brought the party wherever she went. Her motto had always been, "What's done is done."

She greeted Gavin with a big hug. Kyla knew there was some truth to what Tracee had just said, but she would never admit it.

Rollin slapped Gavin on the shoulder. "I'm going to let you guys talk. Gavin, you know where to find me when you finish with your sisters." He walked back into the barn.

Kyla turned to Gavin. "Is everything okay at home?"

He glanced from her to Tracee before nodding. "Everything's cool, why?"

"Because I don't think you've shown up here this early since I've been working here. Mom and Dad are okay?"

"They're fine."

"And the wife and kids?" she continued.

Gavin chuckled. "Donna and the kids are cool. You should come out and see them. They're getting big."

More guilt from her little brother. Kyla nodded. "I will, and soon, I promise. But if it wasn't anything important, I need to run. I'll call you later."

"Naw, go ahead. I'll talk to Tracee. You go kill 'em dead today."

"Good luck girl. I wish I could be there to cheer you on." Tracee leaned over and gave Kyla a hug.

Gavin waved as Kyla hurried back up to the house. She had two hours to get changed and drive to Lexington. She could not be late for her presentation. Besides, Professor Abraham had said he had a surprise for her, and she was eager to see what that was.

After her shower, Kyla dressed in a business suit and heels. She pulled her straight hair back into a French bun. She hadn't allowed herself much time for makeup, so foundation and lip gloss would have to do. She jumped on US 150 and arrived at the conference in time to find Professor Abraham and thank him for the opportunity before grabbing a bottle of water and finding her session. She was the only PhD candidate invited to sit on the panel. The other panelists were business owners or writers who covered the subject of organic farming.

Minutes later, butterflies danced in her stomach as the moderator took the stage, a thin scholarly looking man with thick-framed glasses. He motioned for her group to join them onstage. Kyla made her way to the podium and introduced herself to everyone. Her jittery stomach began bouncing around in overdrive as she glanced around and noticed the room filling up. By the time everyone on the panel was seated across the stage, the room was at capacity.

"Looks like we've drawn a good crowd today," the gentleman next to her said.

Trying to hold the butterflies at bay, she replied, "I just hope I don't forget what I'd planned to say."

"Oh, you'll do fine. The moderator's about to spout off some statistics about the millions of hungry people in America, and then we'll tell everyone what we're doing to reduce that number. It's that simple."

Simple for you. Kyla took a deep breath and looked down at her notes. If she walked out of this room having convinced one or two of the business owners in the crowd to give her nonprofit a try, she would count herself successful.

As predicted, the moderator kicked off the discussion by quoting statistics on world hunger before introducing all five panel members. When Kyla's time came, she went on automatic pilot. She had rehearsed her presentation so much she didn't need to look down at her notes. The more she spoke, the more her confidence grew.

Before she finished her presentation, Kyla noticed quite a few heads turn when two men entered and stood at the back of the room. They were tall, athletic looking and black—and stood out from everyone else here. She tried not to let them distract her as she broke down the specifics of her program and rattled off her accomplishments to date.

"Currently, I'm conducting workshops throughout the Glynn County school system. My goal is to first spread my program throughout the whole state of Kentucky. Then conquer the world." She garnered a little laughter from the crowd. "I'm available after this meeting to speak with anyone about how your church, business or organization can help eradicate hunger right here at home. Or, if you'd be interested in attending one of my workshops at the Coleman Farm to learn more about the food you eat and how we benefit from organically grown foods, I'd be happy to sign you up."

Applause rippled through the room. From her vantage point she could see everything and everyone. People were whispering and turning to look at the men. Kyla figured they were former University of Kentucky athletes, but what were they doing at a World Hunger Day discussion? Someone had brought in folding chairs for them, but they refused to sit down, offering the seats to women standing at the back, instead.

One of the men locked eyes with Kyla, and she tried to place him, but one thing Kyla wasn't was a sports fan. Although she'd been told several times she had the height of a female basketball player, she knew nothing about the sport.

Before she turned away, she had to admit the guy was extremely handsome, and the sight of him almost took her breath away.

"That question was for you, Ms. Coleman," the moderator said into his microphone.

Startled, Kyla sat up straight and looked at the moderator with pleading eyes.

"Would you like me to repeat the question?" he asked.

"Yes, please." She turned her gaze to the back of the room again, where Mr. Athlete was still staring at her.

Oh my God! She quickly averted her gaze and focused on answering the question. A fluttery feeling engulfed her stomach before she realized everyone was staring and waiting on her response.

Chapter 2

"She certainly knows her stuff," Miles Parker whispered to his little brother, Brandon, as they stood in the back of the room at the University of Kentucky's World Hunger Day conference.

"Yeah, but it sounds like a small program," Brandon replied. Brandon had come to spend his summer break with Miles and to learn about running a business. Miles was determined to give his little brother a real-world education before he went back to Georgia State at the end of the summer.

Miles nodded as he continued to listen to the graceful young lady on the panel explain how she'd introduced her nonprofit program, Rooted Beginnings, into the local school system. He crossed his arms, intrigued not only by what she was saying, but also by her. He'd missed the beginning of her presentation and squinted as he tried unsuccessfully to read the name on her badge. She looked like an elegant ballerina sitting on that stage. He had to find out who she was.

The door to the conference room opened with a creak. Miles turned, along with several other people, to see his college mentor, Professor Abraham, with his receding hairline and large black-framed glasses, step into the room. He'd invited Miles to speak and introduce everyone to his company, Parker Edmunds Foods. The moderator took to the podium to close out the session as the professor peered along the back row and spotted Miles. He smiled. Miles smiled in return, happy to see his old friend. The professor made his way along the wall through the crowd.

Abraham reached out his hand. "Miles Daniel Parker, so happy to see you." He spoke loud enough to be heard over the applause going on around the room.

Miles pushed away from the wall and clasped the professor's hand in a firm handshake. "Yes, sir, it's good to see you, too. And thank you for the invitation." Everyone around them was getting up and moving. Miles realized now that he'd missed the pretty young lady's name.

"No, thank you for making room in your busy schedule for our conference. I haven't seen you in quite a while, so congratulations on your retirement from the Chicago Cubs."

"Thank you, but I didn't really have a choice. A bad shoulder and a torn ACL is career ending. But after ten great seasons, I'm not complaining."

"Then it's good you were able to put that business degree to good use. The local media keeps up with your accomplishments. You've really made a name for yourself in the fight against hunger. Makes me proud!"

"Thank you, sir. We're doing what we can with the help of organizations all over the world. I'm always interested in learning about new opportunities springing up in the farming industry. You never know what approach is going to have the most impact."

Brandon cleared his throat.

"Oh, I'm sorry." Miles turned to Brandon. "Let me introduce you to my younger brother, Brandon Parker."

The professor shook Brandon's hand. "Guess I don't have to tell you what a big deal your brother is around here. Two-time All-American Mr. Baseball, and the pride of UK."

Brandon held his chin high and pulled his shoulders back. "Yes, sir, I know. He's made the family proud."

Brandon hadn't played sports in high school. His popularity had come from riding his brother's coattails. Where Miles went, Brandon wanted to go. Miles ran his hand across Brandon's red fro-hawk, which normally freaked him out, but today he merely smiled.

Several people spoke to Miles as they passed. A few reached out to shake his hand and let him know they were big fans. He acknowledged all of them. Visiting the UK campus was always a morale booster. He'd given a lot to the school when he was there, so it felt good to know people hadn't forgotten him.

"So, what's this I hear about you doing some business in the area?" the professor asked.

Miles crossed his arms. "Yes, we're in the process of expanding, so I'm looking for land now. Not right here in Lexington, though. I had something a little more rural in mind."

The professor smiled. "You can take the boy out of the country, but you can't take the country out of the boy."

"Yes, sir," Miles replied with an even bigger smile, not ashamed of his country roots.

The professor looked back over his shoulder before glancing down at his watch.

Miles looked in the same direction, wondering what

had happened to the pretty young lady who'd graced the stage earlier.

"I was looking for a former student of mine. She has a very impressive nonprofit aimed at educating the public about organic foods. I know that's not your area of expertise, but I'd like to introduce you to her."

Miles's eyes widened as a flutter of hopefulness passed through them. "Was she on the stage earlier?" he asked.

"Yes, she was."

"I heard most of her presentation. I'd be happy to meet her. She's very passionate about her program."

"She is. Her name's Kyla Coleman, she's in our PhD program and her nonprofit is part of her dissertation. It's an amazing program and a huge undertaking. You two have something in common."

"Oh, yeah, what's that?"

"The desire to end world hunger on your own terms."

Miles quirked an eyebrow and smiled at the professor. "In that case, I need to make sure I meet this young lady."

Five minutes later, Miles and Brandon made their way down the hall to the conference room where Miles was scheduled to speak.

After reading Miles's bio, the moderator welcomed him on stage. "Ladies and gentlemen, please join me in welcoming the president of Parker Edmunds Foods, Mr. Miles Parker."

Humbled by the introduction and the round of applause, Miles felt overwhelmed in a good way. As he stepped to the podium, the moderator stepped back. This was the first time Miles had been back to his alma mater to speak, but he hoped it wouldn't be the last time.

In the thirty minutes Miles spoke, he briefly explained how Parker Edmunds Foods was making a difference in the lives of hungry people all over the world. He spouted a few statistics he knew would impress the crowd before letting them know his company was expanding, and bringing jobs to the area. He was also open to new ideas and approaches in the fight to end hunger. After his presentation, he took questions from the audience, who were gratifyingly aware of his company and their accomplishments.

Once his forty-five minutes were up, Miles left the stage to another round of applause. The crowd now wanted autographs. He signed numerous ones before being rescued by Professor Abraham and pulled toward the pretty ballerina he'd spotted earlier.

Up close, she was more beautiful than he thought. Her brown skin was smooth and flawless, devoid of heavy makeup. Her natural beauty piqued his interest—as well as his loins.

"Miles, I'd like for you to meet one of my most promising students, Ms. Kyla Coleman."

Miles's chest expanded as he grinned and offered his hand, wrapping it around her elegant slender fingers. "Hello, Ms. Coleman, it's a pleasure to meet you." Her grip was firm.

"Nice to meet you, as well," she said with a pleasant smile.

"I was in the back of the room during your presentation, and I was impressed. You really have a passion for organic farming."

She smiled again, and it set off a fluttery feeling in his stomach that he wasn't used to.

"Yes, I do. You might say it's my life. I found your presentation…interesting, too. Although I'm not actually sold on the benefits of tinkering with the genetic basis of the world's food supply, I appreciate what you're trying to do."

For a brief moment Miles was taken aback, but he quickly recovered and smiled as the professor did the same and stroked his beard.

"That's not all we do at Parker Edmunds. We're a relatively young company being introduced to new approaches in farming all the time."

"But is what you produce beneficial for the community or the environment?" Kyla asked, as she crossed her arms and took on a challenging stance.

Miles glanced at the professor again, and he seemed to be enjoying the conversation. He'd obviously expected this from Kyla, so Miles knew he'd been set up. There were two factions at the conference. Those who dealt in genetically modified foods and those who adamantly opposed them. Both Kyla and the professor were obviously members of the latter group.

Miles cleared his throat. "Check your pantry when you get home, Ms. Coleman. You're probably eating genetically modified organisms, and you don't even know it. However, I didn't come here today to debate the safety of various farming practices. We're here," Miles motioned to Brandon standing a few steps away, "to learn what we can in an effort to expand our global approach."

Kyla smiled at Brandon, and Miles made the introductions as a young volunteer walked over to whisper in Professor Abraham's ear.

"If you'll excuse me, there's a matter I need to attend to," the professor said, as he reached out for Miles's hand. "Miles, please don't leave until I have a chance to sit down with you. Enjoy the rest of the conference."

Then he turned to Kyla. "Young lady, I leave you in capable hands. Miles here is very interested in nonprofit work. Why don't you invite him out to the farm? Show him what he's missing food-wise."

The professor excused himself and dashed out of the room. Kyla glanced around, looking ready to bolt out right behind him, but Miles wasn't letting her get away so fast.

"So, tell me about this farm and your workshops."

Kyla squinted her eyes and tilted her head. "Weren't you listening to my presentation?"

"Unfortunately, we missed the beginning. I assume that's when you talked about the farm."

She hesitated a few moments before going on. "My cousin runs a working organic farm and bed and breakfast a couple of miles from downtown Danville. People come from all over to pick their own organic vegetables and fruits and have our chef prepare them the same day. I joined the staff about a year ago, and I started my nonprofit focusing on clean eating. I teach the benefits of growing your own food, no matter how small or large you start out."

Miles nodded. "Impressive. That sounds like a nice place. And is it cooking classes you give?" he asked with raised eyebrows.

"I teach that what we put in our food, land and water ends up in our bodies. I promote agriculture that is local, a manageable size, humane and socially just. I like to think about our future generations."

Although she was being curt with him at the moment, Miles had a feeling she loved to talk about her work, given the right setting. He tried to ignore the people around them filling up the room for the next session and focus on the astute woman in front of him.

"You know, Ms. Coleman, my knowledge of organic farming is probably not as extensive as yours. And I'd bet the reason you oppose genetically modified ingredients is due to a lack of knowledge on your part. Before the conference is over, maybe we'll each have gained a little more insight into both approaches. One may be as good as the other."

Kyla chuckled and glanced down toward her shoes. "I don't think so, Mr. Parker. It's a one-day event. Maybe you should pay a visit to the Coleman Farm—you might learn something. I'll even let you attend my workshop for free."

"I just might take you up on that," he said, seriously considering it.

The crowd around them grew even larger. Miles knew he had to leave to participate in another discussion down the hall, but the desire to leave Kyla Coleman wasn't there, even though they were at odds. He wanted to get to know her beyond her obvious beauty.

Kyla smiled. "Come on out. I'll be glad to show you around." She pulled her tote bag up onto her shoulder. "Well, it's been nice talking to you. I have another session to attend. Enjoy the conference."

"You, too. It was a pleasure meeting you." Miles quickly reached into his suit-coat pocket and whipped out a business card. "My card, should you ever find yourself in need of our services."

She accepted the card, glanced at it and shoved it into her tote. "Thank you."

As she walked away, Miles followed the graceful sway of her hips until she left the room. She wasn't impressed with him, she might not even like him, but he couldn't shake the feeling that he'd met his match.

Miles signaled to Brandon that it was time to move on. He tore himself away from a group of young female volunteers and joined Miles.

"Why'd you disappear?" Miles asked.

"You and that lady were going back and forth at each other about farm stuff. Man, I wasn't trying to hear all that."

Miles playfully grabbed Brandon by the neck and pushed him in front of him as they walked out of the room. "She invited me out to her farm."

"I don't have to go, do I?" Brandon asked.

"Boy, where I go, you go. I'm trying to teach you about business."

"Looked to me like you had more than business on your mind when you were looking at her."

Miles chuckled. "It's strictly business." What else could it be? he asked himself. Over a year ago, he'd turned his life around and vowed to be celibate until he met the woman he wanted to spend the rest of his life with. He was determined to become a man his father would have been proud of.

Chapter 3

Kyla pushed the covers back and climbed out of bed. Since she'd moved into her cousin's B and B for the summer, the smell of baking bread always woke her in the morning. Her Aunt Rita arrived at 6:00 a.m. to start breakfast, while Tracee usually pulled in around the same time to start baking. With Rita's help, Tracee had stepped up her game since last year, baking pies, cakes, cupcakes, cookies and other gourmet treats that were sold in the new Coleman Farm U-pick store. And on Saturday mornings, like today, everything usually sold out.

Kyla had slept a little longer than usual this morning, and hurried to get showered and dressed in time for the morning tour. Hopefully they'd have a lively group today.

The kitchen was abuzz, with Rita and Tracee whirling around loading plates with fresh fruits, yogurt, organic pancakes, organic eggs and Tracee's mouth-watering organic and vegan banana-almond bread. Kyla joined the whirlwind and grabbed herself a plate.

"Good morning," she greeted her family.

Before anyone could answer her, the kitchen door swung open and Tayler Coleman, Rollin's wife, backed her way into the kitchen with her hands full. "We need more food out there. These boys are gonna eat us out," she said as she set two empty plates on the table. Then she looked up and noticed Kyla. "Morning Kyla."

"Good morning." Kyla loved and respected her cousin Tayler. She could listen to the story of how Tayler came to the B and B for a vacation, fell in love with Rollin and never left over and over again. Kyla wasn't one to believe in fairy tales, but Tayler giving up her corporate VP position in Chicago for the likes of a little country B and B still amazed her.

"We've got us a couple of ballers out there," Tracee said as she handed Tayler two full platters of food. "One said you invited him," she added and glanced over her shoulder at Kyla.

Kyla frowned and looked up from fixing her plate. "I invited him?" she asked, pointing to herself.

"They asked about taking your workshop this morning, so Rollin invited them to breakfast," Tayler added, before she backed out of the kitchen into the dining room.

Kyla frequently invited people out to the farm to see how her program worked. But for the life of her, she couldn't imagine who Tracee meant by *ballers*. Curious, she set her plate down and walked over to the kitchen door, easing it open just a crack.

She could see a few of the guests, but couldn't see who was sitting at the other end of the table. She heard Rollin talking to someone. But that wasn't unusual, since he ate breakfast with the guests on many occasions. Then a voice she recognized made the hair on the back of her neck stand up.

The World Hunger Day Conference was over three weeks ago, but that was definitely Miles Parker's voice.

"Kyla. You okay, honey?" Rita asked.

Kyla let go of the door. "I'm fine."

Tracee crossed her arms and peered across the room at Kyla. "So where did you go to meet a professional baseball player?"

"Wouldn't you like to know." Kyla grabbed her plate and turned to leave the room. "I'll be in the office if anybody's looking for me." She walked down the short hall to the farm's office, and closed the door behind her. Rollin had converted the billiard room into an office big enough for two desks. He'd even purchased her a laptop.

She didn't know whether to be excited, nervous or both. When she'd invited Miles to the farm, she was being polite. She never thought he'd actually show up. She'd assumed his interest in her program was out of sheer niceness to Professor Abraham. What did he stand to gain by taking a farm tour? His business wasn't about organic foods; it was just the opposite.

As the farm's assistant manager, she needed to check her emails and make a few business calls before the morning tour. She attempted to answer some mail, but she couldn't get over the fact that the same Miles Parker she'd seen on the front page of the tabloids in the grocery store was in their kitchen eating breakfast. He was infamous for dating celebrities and seemingly doing whatever it took to get him and his buddies on *Entertainment Tonight*.

A knock on the door snapped Kyla's thoughts back into place.

"Come in."

Tracee walked in and closed the door behind her. "We have an idea. Right now Aunt Rita is in the dining room talking to Miles and his friends. Why don't you get a picture of him while he's here? We can display it in the dining room to show celebrities have eaten here, like they do in restaurants."

Kyla's eyes widened in horror. "I can't ask him to do that. I don't know that man. I met him once, and when I invited him out here, I didn't actually think he'd show up."

Tracee crossed her arms. "Well, he's here. Rollin seems to know him, too. And he and his buddies are loving Rita's breakfast. They ate a whole loaf of my banana bread. He's not a paying guest, so the least he can do is give us a picture."

As if Kyla wasn't already uncomfortable with him being there, now Tracee wanted her to impose on him. She hoped he wasn't the type of celebrity who hated fans requesting pictures. "Okay, I'll ask. Since he knows Rollin, maybe he won't mind. Now get out of here and let me finish these emails."

"I'll get my cell phone and meet you guys out by the truck. I can't believe it, Miles Parker, here!"

"Tracee, don't go out there and make a fool of yourself. Take one picture of him and Rita. That's it."

Tracee turned her lip up at Kyla. "You need to loosen up. You're no fun, you know that?"

"Yes, I am. I'm a lot of fun. Unlike you, I know the difference between work and play."

"Whatever." Tracee walked back to the door. "We'll meet you outside."

Once Tracee left, Kyla shook her head. Her sister acted as if she'd never met a celebrity before. Then again, maybe she hadn't, since Miles was the first celebrity Kyla had ever met. He was not, however, the first player or womanizer she'd ever encountered. Someone from not so long ago came to mind.

She pushed that bad memory from her head and shut down her computer. If it would make Rita happy, she'd ask Miles for a picture.

Kyla grabbed her clipboard and went out the back door to meet Kevin and the truck. Every morning he cleaned the truck up and got it ready for the day's guests. She found him standing at the back of the shiny, pristine vehicle, as usual.

"Them kids yesterday smashed strawberries all over the floorboards," Kevin complained as he finished wiping at some spots. "I swear they got no home training. People need to teach their kids about other people's property."

Kyla opened the passenger door and tossed her clipboard onto the seat. "Kev, you know you love this truck like your own. If it wasn't dirty, you'd still be out here wiping it down."

"Hey, a clean truck is a reflection of the driver. Besides, Mrs. Rollin said we have some special guests this morning, and I don't want them sitting on smashed strawberries." He stopped and looked up at Kyla. "Ever heard of Miles Parker, the baseball player? He went to UK and then played professionally for the Chicago Cubs. I used to watch him all the time."

Kyla rolled her eyes, and rested her hands on her hips. *Geez, did everybody know this guy?* "Yes, I've heard of him." She cut Kevin a quick smile. "What do you say we get started? Our guests are eagerly waiting on the front porch."

Kevin frowned. "Okay, I see what kind of mood you're in this morning. Research not going well?" he asked.

"My research is fine." She climbed up onto the back of the truck and took her usual seat against the back window. "Let's start with collard greens this morning. We can end with cherries. Rita wants to make cherry pies this evening."

Kevin stood at the foot of the truck and smirked. "Yes, ma'am," he said, as he two-finger saluted Kyla.

She rolled her eyes again and shook her head. They

spent so much time together, they were like an old married couple.

As the truck pulled around to the front of the house, an unexpected shiver ran through Kyla when she spotted Miles standing on the front porch smiling and laughing with the other guests. His face lit up, and his square chin softened when he smiled. She wasn't sure why she noticed that. Another thing she noticed was his ultra-bright-white T-shirt, which she would have advised him not to wear had she known he was coming. Where did he think he was going? She'd explained that it was a working farm.

He'd looked effortlessly cool and confident in his suit at the conference, but today, in his casual attire, he was downright hot! The T-shirt showed off his muscular arms and the shorts his nice calves. He had on a baseball cap with a pair of shades sitting above the brim.

The truck came to a halt, and Kyla jumped down to greet the guests and help a few of them up the steps onto the back of the truck. Still standing on the porch with Miles were Tracee, Rita and Tayler, all smiling like a bunch of Cheshire cats. The whole time, her family had been busy taking pictures with Miles.

"Kyla, get on up here and take a picture with us." Tracee waved for her to join them.

Miles turned around, and the corners of his mouth slowly turned up as his eyes widened. He had to be one of the most attractive men she'd ever seen. She stopped what she was doing. "I'll be right back," she said to the guests on the truck before hurrying up onto the porch. Her family was acting starstruck and embarrassing the hell out of her. She had to end this, and quickly.

"Hello, Mr. Parker." She gave him a curt smile and extended her hand.

"Hello, Ms. Coleman. I thought I'd take you up on your invitation," he said as he accepted her hand with a firm shake. "You remember my brother, Brandon? And this is his friend, Trey."

Kyla smiled and shook their hands. Both claimed Miles had dragged them to Danville so early this morning they were just now realizing what was going on. She'd figured as much, from their skinny jeans and bright shirts.

She turned back to Miles. "Well, I didn't expect you but—" she glanced over at her family checking out the pictures on their phones "—welcome to the Coleman Farm. I hear you signed up for the tour this morning?"

Miles rubbed his palms together in an eager gesture. "Yes, ma'am, I'm interested in your program. So I thought I'd come out and see you in action."

For some reason Kyla wanted to blush. She bit her lip and nodded to keep from looking stupid.

"Okay you two, give me a smile." Tracee jumped in front of them with her phone, poised to take a picture.

Suddenly Miles threw his arm around Kyla's shoulder and leaned in like they were old friends. She smiled and tried not to look mortified by the fact that her body tingled all over.

"Got it."

Miles removed his arm, and Kyla took a deep breath. She nodded toward her family. "I hope you don't mind the pictures. They got to you before I could ask."

He shook his head. "Not at all. I'm used to it."

"Thank you."

She then escorted her remaining guests out to the truck. She couldn't keep the self-satisfied grin from her face.

These boys have no idea what they're about to get into.

During the ride out to the green fields, everyone was pretty quiet as they listened to Kyla's pitch about healthy organic eating. She'd chosen the green fields because Rita wanted to serve collard greens for dinner, and they were pretty easy to pick. Every guest was given a basket and a pair of shears. The older guests loved picking the greens and shared stories with Kyla of younger days when they grew vegetables in their yards.

Kyla walked over to Brandon and Trey, who seemed to be picking anything they saw. "You don't want that one," she instructed and took a bunch from Brandon's hand. "See the blemishes on the leaves? No good. You only want greens with no blemishes or withering. These are pretty young, tender greens so you won't find too many bad ones, but skip this one."

"This is the first time they've ever picked a bunch of greens that wasn't already bagged up in the grocery store," Miles said as he joined them.

"Huh, I've never picked up a bunch in the grocery store, either," Brandon said.

"Well, there's a first time for everything, isn't there?" Miles asked.

Brandon shrugged and looked at Trey before they reluctantly continued picking greens.

"I thought you were in the food processing business?" Kyla asked. "You guys have never worked a farm before?"

Miles held up his basket full of greens. "Oh, I have. But it's an introduction for these city boys. I'm trying to teach them a thing or two today." He glanced around. "You have an abundance of greens here. Are all those rows over there greens, as well?"

Kyla looked in the direction he was pointing. "Yes, they are. We have rows of mustard and turnip greens, and kale, as well." When she turned back around, Miles gave her a smile that was disarmingly charming. Her pulse quickened. *Damn, he's good-looking.* She forced her thoughts back to the task at hand.

After the greens they went to pick peppers and then tomatoes before finishing up in the cherry orchard. At every stop, Kyla found herself strolling along talking to Miles.

"Now I wish I could stick around for dinner tonight. Looks like it's going to be good. And I don't know when I've had a homemade cherry pie." Miles plucked a cherry from the tree and popped it into his mouth. "Um, these are sweet."

Thank God he's not sticking around. "Yeah, what Aunt Rita does with these cherries is amazing. Sorry you'll miss out, because as I was saying on the ride over, the cherries are only around to harvest for about two weeks. They're a big hit at the farmers market, and cherries without pesticides—even bigger. People know they're getting quality fruit when they purchase from us." She set her heavy bucket down and dropped the cherries in.

"But how do you keep the bugs off without pesticides? That's not a crop you can produce successfully every year, is it?" He bent over and dumped her cherries into his bucket, handing her the empty, lightweight bucket.

"Bugs aren't a problem, but birds are. So we've planted a few mulberry trees to draw them away from the cherry trees. For a successful production it's all in the soil, and its very labor intensive. These trees are planted on the highest point of the farm with plenty of drainage and good soil depth. The fruit tree roots need water-holding capacity."

"Sounds like you know your fruit trees."

She nodded. "I do, but the farm specializes in vegetables, so we only plant a few fruits. Mind if I ask what your company's interest is in organic foods?" Kyla asked. "Your presentation seemed to center around how you shipped overseas."

"That's not all we do. My partner and I are committed to ending world hunger. We raise money for various groups and take on pet projects from time to time. We started by working on sustainable self-help solutions in third world countries to fight hunger. I'm proud to say we do a lot of good work. 'Think globally, not just locally' is our motto."

"Yes, I remember you saying that during your presentation, as well. I've always liked, 'Each one, teach one,' so I guess you can say that's my motto."

Kyla held her chin high unable to keep the self-satisfied smile from her lips. She wanted Miles to know he wasn't the only one proud of the fruits of his labor. She had a catchphrase of her own. He nodded slowly while holding his bottom lip between his teeth. The look took her breath away.

Chapter 4

After spending the morning in the hot sun, the truck returned to the B and B, where Kevin and Kyla carried the guests' baskets in to Rita. A few of the guests chose to return to their rooms. Those who had signed up for Kyla's workshop waited for her on the front porch.

When Kyla stepped onto the porch, she thanked everyone and then led them to her workshop. Rollin had built Kyla an open-air classroom down the hill from the gift shop. A path led to the gazebo-like structure with mismatched seating that ranged from yard chairs to wooden benches. Flowers and shrubs surrounded the gazebo and a small garden was set off to the right. A sign over the structure read Rooted Beginnings Food Education Workshop.

Kyla helped Rollin secure two interns from the local college every semester. One of the current interns, Ben, assisted with all her workshops. The other, Sean, helped out at the farmers market, which was where Kevin was headed now that he'd dropped them off.

"Morning, Ben," Kyla greeted the young college senior. He wore round, wire-rimmed glasses and had a baby face. He had everything set up and was just waiting for the morning tour to be over.

"Good morning, Kyla. Everything's laid out. I left the—" Ben stopped dead in his tracks, and his mouth fell open.

Kyla followed his gaze and realized he recognized Miles.

"Is that Miles Parker, the baseball player?" he asked.

"Yes, it is. He and his friends are taking the workshop this morning."

"Wow! I never expected to see anybody famous around here. Does he have a farm, too?"

Kyla glanced over at Miles, who seemed to be in a deep discussion with his brother. "I don't know. He said he's interested in organics. I guess we'll see."

"Would it be rude of me to ask him for an autograph?" Ben looked around like he was searching for paper and a pen.

"Ben, let's get some work done first. He's not going anywhere until the workshop is over." Kyla shook her head, amazed at how much people were flipping over Miles.

"Oh, yeah, sorry." Ben walked over to the mobile blackboard he'd set up, along with all the tools needed to maintain a small garden.

After everyone was seated, Kyla moved to the board and began her lecture. "Again, I want to thank everyone for signing up for Gardening Made Simple, brought to you by Rooted Beginnings. Nutrition education empowers people with the tools to make healthy decisions. Before I started my dissertation, I was astonished to find out what some people considered healthy foods. I didn't grow up on an organic farm, but my parents had a little garden out back, and they believed in eating off the land as much as possible. So I guess you can say my introduction to gardening started at an early age."

Out of the corner of her eye she could see Miles staring at her, watching her curiously. The way he hung on her every word made her somewhat uncomfortable. She walked over to the blackboard and began diagramming the bare bones of how to start a simple garden. After the first hour of the lecture, the group moved out into the small side garden she used for demonstrations.

"Everyone grab a pair of gloves. It's time to play in the soil." Kyla pulled her own gardening gloves from the pile Ben had put out for everyone.

Miles had been quiet all through Kyla's lecture, but he walked over to her now.

"I'm not sure if these will do me any good." He held up his hands, showing her the ill-fitting gloves. They were too small for his big hands.

She reached up to one glove, pulling it down so she could examine the tag just inside the wrist—large. He had big strong hands, with large veins in his wrists. "Hmm, looks like we have a situation. I don't have any larger gloves."

"I can just use my hands if you have some place I can wash them afterwards."

"Aw, I'd hate for you to do that, but it's not like gloves are going to protect that pretty white T-shirt of yours anyway," she offered with a sly smile.

"Not to worry," he said quickly, picking up on her joke. "I've got plenty more."

She smiled. "Of course you do."

"Anyway, I'm looking forward to getting my hands dirty and learning everything there is to know about organic gardening. You did say you offer a hands-on approach, correct?"

The way his brows rose with enthusiasm made Kyla

laugh. "It would take years to teach you everything I know, and this is only a ninety minute workshop. How about I focus on the importance of good soil for now?"

Miles stripped the tight gloves off and laid them on the table as he gave Kyla another one of his charming smiles that sent her pulse racing again. "I'm all yours," he said.

Kyla quickly fanned herself as beads of sweat formed across her forehead. She had to turn away from him. "Okay, let's get started."

One of the most important segments of the workshop was for the group to be able to distinguish between soil and dirt. She briefly explained why you get rid of dirt, but preserve soil. She also detailed what soil means to farmers. Then she walked around to see who could tell the difference.

Miles had a handful of each when Kyla walked over to him. She asked him the same question she'd asked everyone else. "You can tell the difference, can't you?" He looked comfortable getting his hands dirty, but she couldn't say the same for Brandon and Trey, who'd barely touched their samples.

"Sure…the dirt's brown, and the soil's black." He gave her a smile that said he was pleased with himself.

Kyla shook her head. "There's more to it than that. The soil is an ecosystem of other organisms." She reached over and took a handful of the soil in front of Miles and held it up. "If you build the perfect soil, your plants will grow and thrive. There's an art to soil building."

Miles dropped the hand full of dirt and held the hand full of soil under hers to catch the soil as she poured it from her hand into his. He gently brushed the remaining remnants of soil from her palm with his fingers. His hands swallowed Kyla's. She wasn't prepared for the shiver that ran down her spine and splintered through her body.

"So, do you think I can learn this art?" he asked.

She quickly pulled her hands away and brushed them together. "Sure you can." She cleared her throat and fought hard not to bite her lip, thus displaying how flustered he'd just made her. "I give a full-day workshop on soil building that you can sign up for. We cover everything from composting to manures, mulching, mushrooms and teas." She recognized the change in pitch of her voice and the fact that she was rambling, so she shut up.

"Tea?" Miles asked.

"Yes, you can fertilize your garden with tea." Why had Kyla found herself spending more time with Miles than anyone else, yet again?

She quickly realized the rest of the group was standing around brushing soil from their gloves and waiting for her to tell them what to do next. She caught Ben's eye and motioned for him to start collecting the gloves. "Excuse me, but it's time to start wrapping up."

She stepped away from Miles and returned to the head of the class. After thanking everyone for giving her ninety minutes of their day, she passed out brochures detailing her other workshops.

Miles stood off to the side of her, holding out his hands. "You know, I could use that place to wash my hands now."

"Oh, Mr. Parker, I forgot, I'm sorry. If you'll follow me I'll show you where you can clean up."

"Right behind you," he said.

They walked up the path toward the back of the house in a leisurely fashion, neither seeming to be in a hurry.

"The tour and the workshop have been amazing so far," Miles said. "I like the working farm concept. I was chatting with a few of the guests, and this is the couple in green's second visit."

"We get a lot of repeat business," Kyla replied as she glanced over at Miles, who licked his lips and smiled. She quickly focused back on the path ahead of them. "Some couples spend every anniversary here. The freshness of the food and baked goods keep them coming back for more."

"So, tell me, what is it you do all day when you're not picking vegetables and building soil?"

Kyla took a deep breath and forced her eyes to stay on the path, and not on Miles. "Well, when I'm not working on my dissertation, I help with marketing and running the farm's office. I've helped arrange monthly specials, like Friday night potlucks, and the B and B celebrates just about everything. I handle most of the social media, also."

"Potlucks? At a B and B?" he asked with a chuckle.

"Sure. The Coleman House is not your typical B and B. During potlucks, people bring food from neighboring farms. It's a real community event. Everyone gets involved. It's fun and organic."

Miles laughed. "That much I gathered."

Once they reached the barn behind the house, Kyla pointed to the inside back corner where Rollin had installed a small vanity made of repurposed material.

Miles washed his hands. "I like this setup back here. It's nice. Don't think I've ever seen a sink in a barn before."

"Rollin's wife had him put it in. I think they used to spend a lot of time out here. Before the farm expanded, there was only the house and this barn. The sink he crafted from an old metal bucket. The handle of the bucket was drilled into the wall with a hand towel hanging from it. I don't know where the old mirror came from above the sink."

He dried his hands on the towel before joining her. "You sound like a busy woman. When do you find time to work on your PhD? Which is pretty impressive by itself, I might add."

Kyla stifled a grin. "Thank you. My studies and the program have taken over my life. When I'm not working, I'm studying. But I'm not complaining. I believe this is what I was put on this earth to do."

"I don't think I've ever met a woman who knew so much about minerals, organic matter and how soil filters water to keep it clean."

Kyla smiled. "You were listening?"

"To your every word." Miles tilted his head and smiled at Kyla.

Damn, there's that smile of his again! She blushed while her stomach did a series of backflips. She was used to guests being intrigued by her work, but this level of inter-est from a celebrity she was not used to, nor her response to his attention. And he kept staring at her, which made her even more self-conscious and puzzled.

"Well, I hope you learned something that will benefit your company." She led the way out of the barn.

"I learned that Professor Abraham was right. You know a lot about organic farming, and you're a great teacher. I like your style."

"Thank you again. You're dishing out so many compli-ments, I'm not sure my head is going to fit under the ga-zebo when I get back."

Before he could respond, his cell phone rang.

"Excuse me. I need to take this."

She nodded. "Sure."

"Hey, Glenda," Miles said as he stepped away.

Unexpectedly, Kyla wondered if Glenda was his girl-friend. From what she remembered, he dated starlets from California to New York, nothing but high-profile models and A-list actresses, of course. She continued to walk down the path and back to the group.

Most of the people had left, but a few had hung back, waiting to speak to her. She answered some questions be-fore Miles returned. His brother and friend waited for him outside the gazebo.

"Ms. Coleman, I'd like to thank you for an enlightening morning. I'm afraid we have to leave, but the experience is one I won't soon forget."

She could tell he'd enjoyed himself by the huge smile on his face. "Hopefully you have a new appreciation for organics now."

Miles chuckled. "Let's say I have a better understanding of the work involved, and I see why you're so passionate about it. I understand the health benefits, but it seems like a mighty slow way to feed large groups of people."

"Organic food can feed the masses. If we had more time, I'd tell you how."

"Another time, then." Miles held out his hand. "Tell your family I said thank you for breakfast and the hospitality."

She accepted his hand. "I will." She looked down at his dirt- and soil-spotted T-shirt. "Next time we'll have large enough gloves or an apron for you to wear."

He smiled and brushed at his soiled shirt.

"Drive safely." Kyla said goodbye and rejoined the group of guests, while Miles and his crew walked up the path to the parking lot. She tried her best not to watch him walk away. Her brush with celebrity had been brief, but entertaining. Yet she still didn't see what all the fuss was about. He hadn't struck her as any different from any of the other country boys running around the area. Maybe he was more handsome and charming, and had perfect teeth, which usually scored high in her book, but those weren't things to get your panties in a bunch about.

Ben walked up next to her. "Are they leaving?"

"Yep," she said, half relieved, and half saddened, for some strange reason.

"Man, I didn't get his autograph or anything. I wanted a picture."

"Ben, he's just a man. Tracee took pictures with her phone. Ask her to send you one."

"Okay, but I wanted a selfie with him." He walked off mumbling, "Man, Miles Parker was here and I didn't even get a picture."

Shaking her head, Kyla turned around to clean up her working area, but couldn't resist the urge to glance up the hill to the parking lot. A large black SUV drove slowly down the long driveway to the main road. She smiled to herself. "Goodbye, Mr. Parker. Maybe we'll meet again sometime."

Exactly a week later, just as the buzz of having a celebrity in the house had all but died down, Kyla walked into the dining room and found a framed photograph of Miles and Rita, smiling from ear to ear. The picture hung above the buffet table.

"Nice, isn't it?" Tracee asked as she strolled in behind Kyla, pushing a dust mop across the hardwood floors.

Kyla crossed her arms. "Huh, the only thing missing is his scribbled autograph across the bottom."

"Yeah, about that. Do you think you'll see him again?" Tracee asked.

Kyla unfolded her arms. "I should think not! It's not like he's one of my buddies or anything. If I ever see that man again, it'll probably be on television coming out of some swanky night club in LA or escorting some starlet on some award show's red carpet."

"Well, the more popular he gets, the better for us."

"And how do you figure that?"

"Because you're going to take one of those pictures I took and put it on our website and Facebook. You can say, 'A typical guest at The Coleman House B and B.'"

Kyla's head jerked back. "Aunt Rita is not going to let us post her picture all over the internet. Besides, don't you have to ask his permission to do something like that?"

"If you knew how to get in touch with him, you could ask."

"Well, I don't."

"Nice picture, isn't it?" Tayler asked, as she stopped at the entrance to the dining room with a hamper full of sheets.

Kyla looked up at the picture again. "You really think so?"

"Of course." Tayler entered the room. "Rita's so proud of it. Her first celebrity. She's thinking about sending a copy to the paper. Rollin told her to go ahead. It might bring a little free publicity our way. I think we can get them to do another feature on the B and B."

Kyla tilted her head, giving the picture one more careful review. Was Miles really that big a deal? And she hadn't seen her Aunt Rita happy about any photo taken of herself in years. She did have Miles's business card in her bag somewhere. Maybe Tayler was right. She shrugged before saying, "I guess I could put up one post."

Tracee cleared her throat and continued dusting the floor around Kyla. "I'll email you the pictures."

Kyla slowly nodded. After all, what harm could it do?

Chapter 5

"Are we sure we want to get in bed with these guys?" Glenda asked.

Miles sat across the table from his business partner, at Saul Good's sandwich shop, and contemplated her question. In the five years he and Glenda Edmunds had been in business together, her instincts had never been wrong. Glenda may have the body of a supermodel, but she also had the brains of a business mogul. The first time they met at a local beer festival he attended with friends, he asked her out. That date turned into a business meeting, and the partnership was formed.

"What about the Latin American deal don't you like?" Miles asked.

"It's too good to be true. I agree we need more public–private partnerships to generate crops that meet the needs of poorer countries, but the study they're citing, I've never heard of this institute." She pushed some papers across the table to him. "Give me a little more time to study them before we all sit down."

He picked up the papers and skimmed over the first page. "Sure, take a few more days."

"Great." Glenda closed her folder and sat back in her seat. "So, how are things going with Brandon?"

After taking a deep breath, Miles rested his forearms on the table's edge and turned his hands palms up. "He's coming along, I guess. It's not quite the summer vacation he planned, but I'm gonna make sure he goes back to school with some real-world business experience."

"How did he like the World Hunger Day conference?"

Miles shrugged. "He got bored and started hitting on some of the young female volunteers."

Glenda laughed. "He's a Parker, all right. Why don't you let him shadow me for a week or so? We can take care of some business, and he can help me shop for a new car."

"Oh, he'll love that. The car part, anyway."

She held her fork up. "Then let's make it happen."

Miles nodded, and they continued to eat. After several bites, Glenda got back to business.

"So, last week when we spoke you were going to check out the property in Nicholasville I was telling you about. What happened with that?"

"It's been a crazy week. I haven't had time to run back down there."

"I thought you were already in the area? You said you were in Danville."

"I was actually on a working organic farm in Danville."

Glenda put her fork down, laughing, and wiped her mouth with a napkin. "You worked on an organic farm? What on earth for?"

"At the conference, my college mentor introduced me to this woman who has a nonprofit program called Rooted Beginnings that focuses on organic fruits and vegetables.

She's already gotten her program into the local school system. She's pretty sharp."

Glenda leaned back in her seat and crossed her arms. "Oh, I get it now. What's her name?"

"Kyla Coleman. She's working on her PhD. And what is it that you get, exactly?" he asked before taking another bite of his burger.

"Why Miles Parker would spend *any* time on a farm."

Miles straightened his back. Glenda knew him better than anyone. He wasn't the type of guy who planted his own anything. He purchased everything from the grocery store or had the store deliver. She also knew he wasn't the womanizer the gossip rags made him out to be. "Glenda, you know me better than that. Her program sounded like something I might be interested in, so I decided to check it out."

"Miles, dial it back. You're talking to me. We deal in drought-resistant soybean seeds, not organic fruits and vegetables. Unless you're thinking about investing in another business?"

"No, of course not. But I like to remain open to everything. During her presentation, she mentioned something about a new method in farming. I was hoping to learn more, but she didn't get into that."

"So what did you learn?"

"That she places a large emphasis on food education. It was interesting."

Glenda leaned forward. "In other words, nothing, when you should have been checking out that fourteen-acre farm in Nicholasville. I'm telling you, it's going up for foreclosure, and we need to grab it."

Miles wiped his mouth with a napkin. "I'm thinking about going back down there for a week, so I'll check it out then."

Glenda's eyes widened. "Are you serious?"

"Yes, I am. The farm is also a B and B. The owner, Rollin Coleman, is a former football player from UK. He was there at the same time I was. It's a nice place. Besides, in half a day's time I didn't get to see much of what she does."

Glenda exhaled a long breath and looked down at the table. Then she inhaled and raised her head. "Miles, I hope it's the farming you want to get up close and personal with, and not something else."

Finished eating, Miles pushed his plate aside. "Glenda, I'm all about business. If anybody knows that by now, it's you."

Glenda also pushed her plate aside just as the waiter came to clear the table. After he walked away she said, "I know, you've been more focused than ever lately. It's ultimately up to you, but I don't think I'd stay a whole week. A day or two, maybe. What do you hope to learn in a week's time?"

A little voice in the back of Miles's head told him to listen to Glenda, but his instincts shut that voice up. "Something that will take our business to the next level. You know how we stumbled across that microfinancing connection?"

Glenda nodded.

"Well, if my instincts are any good, our next business venture might be right there waiting for me to come digging in the dirt."

After Miles had his assistant book him a room at the B and B under an assumed name, she'd informed him that the photo he'd authorized via email of himself and the cook was posted proudly on their website. He smiled when he thought about that day as he headed back to the B and B to spend some more time. The only thing that mildly worried him now was not being able to monitor Brandon for a week, but Glenda had assured him she had everything under control.

Miles arrived at the B and B on a Sunday evening just past sunset. He grabbed his duffel bag from the backseat of his SUV and walked up to the front porch. Two guests had taken up residence in the large white rocking chairs that flanked the front door.

"Good evening, folks," Miles said in greeting.

"Evening, sir." An elderly man in wire-rimmed spectacles holding a glass of what looked like whiskey, but was probably iced tea, returned the greeting.

"Good evening." The woman across the porch with knitting yarn and needles in her lap spoke without looking up.

Miles smiled at the Norman Rockwell-ish scene and opened the front door. He walked into the foyer and immediately smelled something baking. He didn't know if it was apple pie, banana bread or a combination of both, but it smelled wonderful. The first time he'd visited, he had two young men with him who took most of his attention. This time, the grandness of the foyer caught his eye the minute he walked in. He was reminded of several classic films he'd watched that were set in the South.

He strolled over to the front counter while marveling at the staircase that was unlike anything he'd seen in a typical Southern home. No one was around, so he tapped the little silver bell on the desk. He turned around and leaned against the counter.

So, this is my home for the next five days. Nice. The Coleman House B and B wasn't as posh as some hotels he'd stayed in, but this was pure Southern charm.

The hall door opened, and a beautiful black sister came out to greet him.

"Hello, thank you for visiting The Coleman House. Are you checking in?" she asked.

"Yes, I have a room reserved for the week." He blinked,

almost forgetting his false name. "Uh, Frank Meeks," he finally said with a smile.

She tapped his name into the computer. "Yes, Mr. Meeks, we've been expecting you. Are you alone?"

"Yes, just me for the week."

"Well, it says here you're paying by credit card, so if I can see the card we'll get you all checked in."

While Miles fished the card out of his pocket, the young lady kept talking.

"Are you in town for a special occasion or visiting the college, maybe?"

He shook his head and handed her his credit card. "No."

She looked at the card and then back up at the computer before her brow creased. "I'm sorry, but the name on the card and the name I have here," she touched her computer screen, "don't match."

He leaned on the counter. "Yeah, about that. I had my assistant make the reservation in another name, if you don't mind, to protect my privacy while I'm here. I'm here to do a little research."

Her eyes narrowed. "Research? What kind of research?"

Before he could answer, the door opened again and a woman he recognized, but whose name he couldn't remember, walked out.

"Mr. Parker!" she exclaimed.

Miles straightened and smiled. "Hello. I'm back."

"Corra, this is Miles Parker, the baseball player in the picture with Rita." The woman who'd come to Miles's rescue now held out her hand. "Remember me? I'm Tayler, Rollin's wife. We took a picture together, too. I'm the one who used to live in Chicago."

Miles raised his chin and accepted her hand. "Yes, I remember. Tayler, it's nice to see you again." The introductions during his first visit had been brief, but he remembered her face.

"You're checking in?" Tayler asked with wide eyes.

"Frank Meeks is checking in," Corra corrected, then winked at Tayler.

"Although it's not always necessary, I sometimes use an assumed name in order to get a little privacy. I want to spend some time learning about Rooted Beginnings and the rest of the farm."

"Oh, sure, not a problem." Corra continued signing him in. "My husband used to play football for the University of Kentucky. Maybe you've heard of him, Christopher Williams?"

Miles took a step back and chuckled. "Of course I know Chris. He was an upperclassman when I was at UK. That's right, he's from around here, isn't he?"

"Yep, he grew up in Danville," Corra replied. She handed Miles his credit card back.

"Man, it would be great to see him before I leave." He put the card back into his pocket.

"He's out of town right now, but I'm sure I can make that happen as soon as he returns," Corra said with a smile.

"That would be great."

Tayler came from behind the counter. "Let me show you to your room. I hope you'll find it acceptable."

"Thank you." He quickly turned back to Corra. "It was a pleasure meeting you, and I look forward to catching up with Chris this week."

She smiled. "The pleasure was all mine."

Miles picked up his bag and followed Tayler up the grand staircase.

"You don't have to worry about your privacy. We're very good at keeping our guest list from prying eyes."

"Thank you. I usually don't do things like this by myself, so I kind of want to enjoy the experience. I can't believe Rollin and Chris are both affiliated with this B and B."

"Seems like a reunion for you guys." Tayler stopped at

the first door on the right at the top of the stairs. With a key, she opened the door and walked in. "This suite has a king size bed and looks out onto the gardens out back. It's cozy, but it has all the modern conveniences." She opened the bathroom door and turned on the light. "I think you'll find everything you need in the bathroom."

He walked into the room and dropped his duffel bag next to the bed. "This is great." The room was nicely decorated in neutral colors and came with a four-poster bed, a fireplace, and a small desk and chair perfect for his laptop, if he bothered to pull it out this week. He walked over and peeked into the bathroom, happy to see a shower large enough for him.

Tayler stood in the room's entrance. "Well, there's herbal tea and cookies in the dining room if you're interested. Breakfast starts at seven, and the truck leaves at eight. You've experienced that before, so you know what to expect."

He smiled at her, happy with the hospitality and the fact that she didn't ask him a lot of questions. "That's the reason I'm here."

"I bet Kyla will be surprised to see you in the morning. She's out right now."

He felt an unexpected warmth at the mention of her name. "I hope I'll be a good surprise."

"Oh, I'm sure you will be," Tayler said with raised brows. "Well, we have an extensive library if you want to kick back and read something or watch a movie. As soon as Rollin returns, I'll let him know who Frank Meeks really is," she said with a wink before leaving Miles alone.

He sat down to test out the bed. It was nice and comfortable. The size of the room reminded him of his bedroom growing up, only he didn't have his own bathroom. He took off his shoes and fell back across the bed to stare up at the ceiling. Why had he decided to take a week out of his busy life to stay in this small-town B and B picking organic vegetables? He was interested in Kyla's pitch from a business perspective, but did he really need to get his hands dirty?

If he was being honest with himself, maybe Glenda was right and there was more to his visit than research.

Chapter 6

On Monday morning, Kyla climbed out of bed in a great mood, hurried through her usual routine of showering and then throwing on her uniform.

Breakfast at The Coleman House was the busiest time of the day. The usual smell of bread baking and tea simmering made Kyla's stomach grumble. She greeted her family before grabbing a muffin off a platter on the kitchen table. This morning she was hungrier than usual.

Tayler popped into the kitchen from the dining room, balancing two empty plates in one hand and a pitcher of orange juice in the other.

"You!"

Kyla jumped.

"What time did you come in last night?" Tayler demanded, as she deposited the plates in the sink and the pitcher on the kitchen counter.

"I don't know. Not too late, why?" Kyla took a bite of her muffin. Tayler's tone surprised her. They hadn't insisted she come in at any particular time since she'd moved in. Was she in trouble?

Tayler crossed her arms. "Because we waited up for you, that's why."

Stumped, Kyla glanced around the room. They'd never waited up for her before. "Is something wrong?" she asked.

Rita walked in from the back hall, clearing her throat and looking in Tayler's direction. Something was going on.

"No, everything's okay. Rollin just wanted to talk to you, but it can wait until around lunch," Tayler answered, after she glanced over at Rita.

Kyla glanced from Tayler to Rita, who had started humming as she loaded the dishwasher. "Okay, I'll look for him."

"Well, breakfast is over and the guests are waiting on the front porch, so you'd better get going," Tayler said, walking over to help Rita clean the kitchen.

"Okay." Kyla decided to play along. Tayler had never rushed her out of the house before. She left the kitchen and grabbed the clipboard from the hall with the names of all the guests for today. She walked out the back door shaking her head. *Those ladies are up to something.*

Kevin had the truck parked in its usual spot and was currently sweeping the bed with a broom.

"What we got this morning?" he asked as Kyla approached.

She read through the list then tossed the clipboard into the passenger's seat.

Kevin secured the broom under the seats and jumped down from the truck bed as she climbed up, taking her seat on the bench below the rear window.

"Let's get this show on the road," he said before climbing into the truck and starting it up.

They drove to the front of the house to pick up the guests, and Kyla jumped down the minute Kevin stopped.

She lowered the back step to help an elderly couple who'd been with them a week now.

Kyla was on autopilot—until the front door opened and an unexpected guest walked out.

Every muscle in her body stiffened as Miles Parker stepped out the front door ahead of Rollin. They shook hands before Rollin walked off and Miles strolled toward the truck. Kyla took a long, deep breath to slow her racing heartbeat and regain control of her senses. What was *he* doing here? Now she understood the strangeness in the kitchen earlier.

Dressed in brown cargo shorts, a navy blue polo shirt and a pair of hiking boots, he looked ready to go to work. She quickly walked back over to the passenger door, opened it and reached inside for the clipboard.

"What's wrong?" Kevin asked.

She read through the list thoroughly, not finding Miles's name. "I'm not sure. This guy's not on the list." When she turned back around, Miles stood at the foot of the truck, speaking with one of the guests.

Kyla joined them. "Excuse me—"

"Good morning, Kyla," Miles said with a big smile.

"Morning. Unless I'm missing something—"

"Frank Meeks," he interrupted her again.

"What?" she asked.

"That's the name I registered under. I'm Frank Meeks—" he lowered his voice "—this week, anyway."

Kyla cautiously glanced back down at the clipboard. Frank Meeks was on the list. He'd checked in yesterday.

She took a deep breath and studied Miles as he casually rested his elbow against the side of the truck, still smiling. "Would you like to be addressed as Frank?" she asked.

He shook his head. "No, Miles is fine. I'm so used to staying in large hotels where the guests list gets out and all sorts of strange people start hanging around. I was trying to protect myself from that, but now that I'm here, I don't think it's going to be a problem."

She tossed the clipboard back into the truck and closed the door. "Well, welcome back. If you'll have a seat in the truck, we'll get started."

"Yes, ma'am." Miles turned around and joined the rest of the group in the truck.

Kyla looked inside at Kevin sitting behind the wheel. He had a big grin on his face as he mouthed the word *Wow*. She shook her head, unable to believe what was happening this morning. Why had Miles Parker come back to the B and B as a paying guest? It meant he'd slept there last night and would be sticking around all week, according to him.

She composed herself and joined the group in the back of the truck. Once she welcomed everybody and recited the usual truck rules, she tapped on the window, letting Kevin know they were ready to go.

As the truck traveled down the road, Kyla went into education mode, discussing the choice of crops they would see today, and then entertained questions. Occasionally, she glanced in Miles's direction, noticing how comfortable he seemed on a bench too narrow for his ass. He didn't ask any questions; he only crossed his arms and observed. The group seemed oblivious as to his celebrity status.

The truck pulled to its first stop, the vegetable garden. Everyone was given a basket and was instructed where to start. Miles hung back after the rest of the group strolled away.

"Mr. Parker, did you have a question?" she asked.

"I did, actually. If it's not too much to ask, I'd like to shadow you for the week. If I won't be getting in the way, that is."

She swallowed hard. "Uh, well… I, uh—" She glanced into the truck at Kevin, who had his cell phone glued to his ear, yammering away, before turning back to Miles.

"I suppose it won't be a problem. I don't do anything too exciting," she said with a wrinkle of her nose.

"You said if you had more time, you'd tell me how organic food could feed the masses. I'm interested in learning how."

Kyla hadn't expected this from a GMO man. Could he be having second thoughts about the damage his company did to the world? Maybe her presentation had had a life-altering effect on him. Then again, maybe not, but she was about to do her best to convert him in a week's time.

"I'm glad to hear that, Mr. Parker. And what better way to learn why sustainable farming is so beneficial than the hands-on approach? Which means I'm going to work your butt off." She knew she had a grin the size of the Grand Canyon on her face, but she couldn't help it. "And I hope lectures don't bore you, because during the summer I do a lot of that."

Miles laughed. "No, I'm sure I won't be bored at all. I'm here to learn, so work me in any way you see fit. Frankly, I'm looking forward to it."

Miles quirked a brow and smiled at Kyla, causing a quiver in her stomach. He reached out his hand, and like a robot, she gripped it in a firm handshake.

"By the way," he said. "You don't have to keep addressing me like I'm some older man. Just Miles, okay?"

She nodded. "Okay then, Miles."

Kyla stood there as Miles, with his muscular legs and arms, walked toward the rows of vegetables holding a small bushel basket and looking out of place. What had just happened? *Did I really agree to let Miles Parker, the playboy of professional baseball, follow me around for a whole week?*

"So, how goes it?" Kevin asked when he popped up next to her.

Her head whipped around so fast she made herself lightheaded. "Do you have to talk on the phone all the time?" she asked through clenched teeth. "I needed you out here and you were on the phone again."

Eyes wide, Kevin shrugged. "What did I miss?"

"That guy is going to be here all freakin' week. He wants to shadow me, for Christ's sake."

"For real?"

"Yes, and he makes me nervous."

"Why? Aside from the fact that he's rich and famous."

Kyla crossed her arms. "That doesn't impress me. It's the hovering I'm not sure I'm going to like."

"Or maybe it's that celebrity athlete charm that has you nervous. Afraid you'll fall under his spell?" Laughing, Kevin flexed his fingers in Kyla's face.

She smacked at Kevin's hands until he stopped.

After Miles's first visit, Kyla had Googled him. There was no denying his wealth and fame, which she already knew. And there were a slew of women who'd attached themselves to him over the years. But she hadn't seen any recent articles about him and any woman. All the recent search results were about Parker Edmunds or his philanthropic endeavors.

"The only thing his charm is going to get him this week are blisters. He wants to shadow me and I can use another pair of hands. I hope Mr. Baseball brought his A game, because he's going to need it."

After the morning truck ride and after she'd deposited all the food in the kitchen, Kyla moved on to the next chore. She walked out the back door and followed the path past the gift shop, waving to Corra as she opened it up. At the end of the path, the doors were open on a small barn where the interns were busy inside setting up for the day.

Kyla loved the cute little barn that Rollin had built for Tayler after their wedding. Since the U-pick store was all her idea, he did everything he could to support it. Above the door, Kevin had hung a sign that read, Coleman Farm, A Labor of Love.

The minute Kyla walked into the barn, Ben came running over.

"Hey, Kyla, is it true that Miles Parker is back?" Ben's eyes widened with excitement.

She nodded. "Yes, he's here. And now you can get your autograph."

"I heard he's staying all week! He must have been impressed with your workshop, huh?"

Kyla laughed. "I doubt that. If anything, he didn't see enough in half a day. Which is why he's back, to learn more." She tried to walk around and check the inventory, but Ben followed her every step and kept asking about Miles.

"I guess you guys have a lot in common, since he has a food company, too?" Ben asked.

"We don't have anything in common," she said. Then she noticed Ben looking over her shoulder and smiling, so she slowly followed his gaze.

"But we do have something in common," Miles said from behind her. "My company wants to feed the world, just as you do."

"Hi, Mr. Parker, I'm Ben." Ben wasted no time shoving his hand at Miles. "Remember me from the workshop a couple of weeks ago?"

"Hello, Ben. Yes, I do remember you. How's it going, man?"

Ben grinned so big, Kyla bet his face hurt.

"I'm hanging in there. If you don't mind, can I get your autograph before you leave?"

"Sure, not a problem. Just keep it to yourself for about a week if you don't mind."

"Okay, sure not a problem. Well, I'd better go help Sean finish setting up."

Before he walked away Kyla asked, "What are we low on?"

Ben looked back at the tables with baskets of fruits and vegetables. "Tomatoes. Those are always the first to go."

"Okay." Kyla turned back to Miles. "You did say you wanted to shadow me, right?"

Miles rubbed his palms together and smiled. "That's right. I'm all yours."

"Ben, would you get us a couple of large containers? We're going to pick some tomatoes."

As Ben walked away, Miles glanced around with a confused expression on his face. "I thought this barn was open for locals to come pick their own vegetables?"

"Oh, it is. However, we always have a fair amount already picked for those who choose not to go out into the fields." She noticed a slight drop in Miles's shoulders.

"I see." Miles took a deep breath and licked his lips. "So, you're sending me back out into the fields?"

"Yep," Kyla said with a smile. "That's what hands-on experience is all about."

Ben returned with two large blue containers. Kyla knew it was a bit much to ask of Miles, but shadowing her meant he'd have to work. She took one of the containers from Ben and held it out to Miles. He looked at the container with wide eyes. "That's a pretty big container for tomatoes."

"Yeah, we like to fill up at least two or three for the day. If that's too large for you I can—"

He accepted the container. "No, it's cool, I've got it," he said, smiling at Ben.

Kyla waved at Tayler, who was busy opening the cash register for the day. Then she pulled out her phone and texted Kevin to come pick them up.

"After the tomatoes we'll do a little weeding. It's very

time-consuming and tedious, but that's what organic farming is all about."

Miles grinned and shook his head. "Five days of this is what I signed up for, didn't I?"

Kyla beamed. "Yes, you did. Around here we don't have a lot of machines to do all the work. As the sign out front says, it's a labor of love. Hope you're ready to get dirty."

"I'm ready for anything," he replied.

"I certainly hope so," she said, half under her breath, as she turned and strutted out to wait for Kevin.

Only time would tell if he could keep up with the pace around here—time that would be largely spent in her company.

Kyla didn't know how to feel about that.

Chapter 7

Harvesting tomatoes wasn't too bad, but manually weeding the garden beds wasn't exactly what Miles thought he would be doing this week. The labor-intensive work, along with the hot sun beating down on them, made those rocking chairs on the B and B's front porch look better and better by the minute.

Kyla had thrown on a large sun hat and was down in the dirt yanking weeds like there was no tomorrow. He'd never met a woman that beautiful without an ounce of vanity about herself. Beads of sweat rolled down the side of her face, and for some reason that looked so sensual to him. At the conference she'd worn her hair up in a bun, but here she wore it pulled back into a low ponytail, swinging down her back. He bet she was stunning with her hair down.

Kyla looked over at Miles, and he smiled, then returned to yanking pesky weeds from the ground.

"Getting hot?" she asked.

He shook his head. "I'm good. How about you?"

"I'm hot, I'm tired and I'm thirsty."

"Wanna take a break?" he asked.

She looked around before wiping her forehead with the short sleeve of her polo shirt. "Let's finish this row first."

Miles glanced up ahead. His particular row had to be another twenty feet, if not more. "Okay, how about I race you?"

She laughed. "What? As hard as this is, you want to race?"

He shrugged. "It's not so bad. Let's see who finishes first." He had to do something to take his focus off the perspiration rolling down her beautiful face.

She smiled like she knew something he didn't and then bit her bottom lip. He got the impression he was in trouble.

"Okay, let's go."

Miles applied laser focus to the weeds in front of him. Sweat drenched his face, his back and under his T-shirt. He yanked, plucked and tossed, but somehow she finished before him.

She threw her hands up. "Ta-da! The winner and weeding champ, Kyla Coleman."

Miles threw his weeds in the bag and sat down in the dirt. How in the hell had she beat him? She joined him, grinning like she'd won the lottery.

"A little harder than you thought, huh?" she asked in a patronizing tone.

"Let's just say, it's not quite what I expected. You don't have machines for this?"

"We do, but they're only used if we miss the window of opportunity. Which is now, while they're small." She squatted down across from Miles and started pulling up weeds. "Come on, I'll help you finish this row."

"I have a feeling this week is going to be a real eye-opener," he said, as he continued to wrap his big hands around the base of the little weeds and yank.

"I thought you worked on a farm before?"

"Nope. I have some knowledge of the industry, of course. Growing up, my parents had a very small garden out back that I was forced to help with."

"Forced!" Kyla said with a laugh.

"Yeah, I was into sports. I didn't want to be in the backyard pulling up onions and picking green beans."

Kyla stopped and looked at him. "So, where are you from, and how did you wind up in the food distribution business?"

He took a deep breath. "I'm from Douglasville, Georgia. And you might say my calling, as I refer to it, started in middle school. My parents were missionaries, so we lived in West Africa and parts of the Caribbean until I was in high school."

"What did they do over there, teach Christianity?"

"They did the Lord's work through our church. My father's focus was on sustainability. He raised money and helped villagers in need. Everything I saw had a lasting impression on me."

"That's where you saw all the hunger, right?"

"Yeah. The devastation was overwhelming. I wanted to go home and send them all my food. Later on, I learned there are numerous reasons the food doesn't get to the people. It's crazy. And there's so much political red tape. It's extremely frustrating. But the smiling faces on the people you do help keeps you doing whatever you can."

Kyla returned to pulling weeds. "I know what you mean. I did an internship in Panama. It was eye-opening, for sure. But then I came home and saw a news story about hunger in rural America. For some kids, the school lunch is their only meal of the day. I couldn't imagine that kind of poverty right here in my own backyard."

Miles had reached the end of the row. Kyla tossed the

last of her weeds into the bucket. He understood her passion and believed she was capable of so much more.

"So, after your internship, you started Rooted Beginnings?" he asked.

"No. I took a job as a food marketing expert in Maryland." Kyla motioned for Miles to bring the bucket of weeds and follow her. "I enjoyed the work, but all it did was make me want to learn more and help more. Sitting behind a desk all day wasn't what I wanted to do. I needed to touch people, you know?"

"I think I know what you mean. Just like I hate to deal with the red tape that slows my seeds from getting where they need to be."

Kyla took off her hat and wiped the sweat from her brow. "Feeding people feeds my soul, as well. Especially the knowledge that what I'm doing is good for them."

He sighed. "Durable and drought-resistant seeds feed a lot of people. What I'm doing is good for people, too."

Kyla gave him a smug smile and turned, walking toward a makeshift stand that held the buckets of weeds. Miles knew they might have some disagreements this week, but he had faith they'd find some common ground.

"Kyla, I know you have a problem with my company's approach to ending hunger, but I'm not here to convert you this week."

Scratching the back of her head, Kyla asked, "What are you really here for?"

Miles set his bucket down and crossed his arms. "You know what I'm here for."

She shook her head. "No, I don't, because from the articles I've read on the internet, you're more the partying type, hanging out with rappers and models, than an astute businessman."

He threw his arms up. "Don't tell me you believe everything you see on the internet. You're basing your opinion of me on some stories meant to get ratings. Do I like to go out and party? Some of the time, yes. Do I date beautiful women? Sometimes, yes. But I'm also a responsible young man. Don't believe everything you read."

Kyla threw up her hands, mimicking him. "Okay, I get it. Not all the stories about you stumbling out of clubs and hanging with supermodels are true."

Miles drew in a deep breath and released it. "I've never stumbled out of any club. Instead of *Googling* me, get to know me before you form an opinion." The frustration of being perceived in the wrong light yet again was irritating, but he hadn't meant to come across so harsh, and from her wide-eyed expression, she hadn't expected it, either.

She let out a long, low sigh.

"So, teacher, can we get off to a better start?" he asked, holding out his hand.

He liked the way her face transformed from a pinched expression to a softer, happy one. Before the week was out, he'd have her smiling all over the place. She finally accepted his hand.

"Kyla, I have a feeling this week is going to be educational for the both of us."

After the morning chores, Miles took a quick shower and freshened up. When he walked back downstairs, the smell of fresh-baked cookies filled his nostrils. Mrs. Rita and Tayler stood in the dining room setting out plates of baked goods. Two huge pitchers sat at one end of the table.

"Mr. Parker, help yourself to some of my famous lemonade or a little refreshing cucumber water." Rita gestured to the goods on the table. "These are Tracee's homemade soft-baked chocolate chip cookies."

"First of all, ladies, please call me Miles. And how did you know I love chocolate chip cookies?"

The ladies turned to each other and said in unison, "Who doesn't?"

Miles bit into the soft, warm cookie, and the chocolate sweetness exploded in his mouth. "This has to be about the best chocolate chip cookie I've ever tasted, and I'm particular about my sweets," he said. "And it's still warm."

Rita unfolded her arms. "Help yourself, Miles. There's more where those came from." She spun around and returned to the kitchen.

"So this is part of the B and B's ambiance, warm baked cookies. I like it." Before he took another bite, he took a sip of the lemonade. It wasn't too sweet or too tart. It was perfect.

"This is the bomb. Perfect after a long morning in the sun."

Tayler laughed. "This morning was nothing. If you're shadowing Kyla, you're going to spend hours in the sun. She works hard. I don't know what we'd do without her around here."

"Yeah, she's breaking me in like a horse."

"Well, you told her you wanted to learn about organic farming, and that's her passion. I'm surprised she doesn't have you out there right now."

"After we finished weeding what felt like the whole vegetable garden, she said she had to make a delivery. She's going to introduce me to the greenhouse when she returns."

"Kyla is by far the smartest young lady I've ever met. She's very knowledgeable about the farm. She does a little bit of everything around here. One day you might find her stringing cucumbers, and the next day she's teaching kids how to grow vegetables. She even helps out around the B and B from time to time," Tayler added.

"Sounds like she's a regular Jack, or Jill, of all trades."

Tayler looked toward the kitchen door and frowned.

"She is. But I wish she'd get out more. She's too young to not have a social life."

Miles nodded, not sure what she expected him to say.

Tayler chuckled. "I don't know why I'm telling you this. But when you're working with her this week and she seems very rigid and controlling, just remember underneath all that agriculture talk is a fun, intelligent woman."

"I don't doubt that. If I'm lucky, she'll let me see that side of her before the week is out."

"Maybe," Tayler replied. "Well, I'll let you enjoy your break. The laundry awaits."

Miles said goodbye, and Tayler left the dining room. That had been a rather interesting conversation, he had to admit. He grabbed another cookie before walking across the hall to the library. A large flat-screen television hung on the wall. He made himself comfortable on the sofa and found a baseball game to watch until he heard someone clear their throat. He turned around. Kyla stood in the doorway.

"I came to see if you wanted to help with the herb garden in the greenhouse, then I realized you might be hungry. Since most of our guests are usually out at this time, we only prepare lunch by special request."

He turned the television off and set the remote down. "I had some of Mrs. Rita's famous lemonade and some warm cookies, but I could use a plate of some protein before I get back to work." He stood up. "And seeing how I don't know my way around Danville, how about you escort me someplace?"

Her eyes widened. "There's a good Mediterranean café in town that you can't miss if you just—"

He walked toward her, shaking his head. "I'm not good with directions, and unless you want me to get lost, you'll go with me." He turned a pair of pleading eyes on her.

* * *

Sitting across the table from Kyla at the café, Miles was once again astonished at how naturally beautiful she was. She didn't need a drop of makeup. Her silky-smooth complexion was enhanced by her long eyelashes and perfectly shaped brows. He noticed she'd added a little spicy-colored lip gloss.

"How's your food?" Kyla asked, after he'd taken a few bites of his Philly cheesesteak gyro.

He nodded. "It's good. Fresh."

She smiled. "We supply their fresh produce every day."

"Really! Do you supply most of the restaurants in town?"

"Only a few. So I like to patronize them when I can."

"Understandable. I can't remember if I already asked you this, but what is it you hope to do with your PhD after you finish school?" Miles found himself taking in every movement and gesture Kyla made. When she ran her hand along the side of her hair before answering him, he marveled at how seductive that slight movement was.

"Initially, I wanted to work for the government. But in Maryland, I worked with this afterschool program that opened my eyes to a lot of things. I realized I wanted to work with children. Most school systems do such an inadequate job of teaching nutrition."

"Do you plan on striking out on your own?"

"My program is nonprofit and I want to keep it that way. So I'll have to get a job in the private sector. I meet a lot of people in my industry, so I hope getting a job won't be hard."

Miles nodded. "Speaking at the conference helped to get your name out there."

"Yeah, but I'd like to make it to the Global Summit on Food and Beverages this year. I'm trying to talk Rollin into signing the farm up, but so far he's not interested."

Miles set his gyro down and wiped his mouth. "I'm speaking at the Food and Beverage conference this year. Or, rather, my company is presenting."

Kyla's eyes lit up, and she set her sandwich down. "Are you kidding me?"

He laughed. "No, I'm not. My business partner loves the networking."

"Wow, that's why I want to go. Imagine all the networking I can do for my program. I don't want to just focus on Kentucky. I want to branch out all over the United States."

"Why not the world?" he asked.

"I believe in starting at home."

"But attending a Global Summit would definitely broaden your perspective. It's in Chicago this year. Have you ever been there?" he asked.

"No, but I bet it's your home away from home, isn't it?"

"You can call it that. I lived there for eleven years. There's no place like Chicago and Wrigley Field. Cold in the winter, but the summers are beautiful."

Kyla picked up her sandwich. "If you don't mind me asking, why did you move back to Kentucky?"

"I still have my condo in Chicago, but Lexington's always been good to me. It feels like home. Besides, it's where I met my business partner and we started our company."

Just as Kyla bit into her sandwich, a tall, older gentleman of Greek heritage approached the table.

"Kyla, welcome!" He held his arms out. "What a pleasure."

Miles wiped his hands as Kyla stood and the man embraced her in a friendly hug.

"Anthimos, it's so good to see you!"

She gestured toward Miles, then clasped her hands together like she didn't know what to do with them. "This is Miles, a guest at the B and B."

Miles stood and accepted Anthimos's offered hand.

"Miles, it's a pleasure. How was your food today?"

"It was great, thank you."

"We serve nothing but the freshest food. All our produce comes from the Coleman Farm."

"Yes, Kyla told me. I probably picked some of these tomatoes myself this morning," Miles added with a slight chuckle.

"Oh, they have you out working the farm." Anthimos elbowed Miles, and nodded toward Kyla. "This one isn't working you too hard, is she? I hear she can be pretty tough."

Kyla crossed her arms. "Anthimos, no, I'm not. Where did you hear that?"

"Ah, word gets around. But as long as I keep getting my fresh produce, you can be as hard as you want." He winked and elbowed Miles again. "This one's a real beauty isn't she?"

Kyla's eyes popped, and she looked like she wanted to crawl under the table.

Miles and Anthimos were definitely on the same page about that, but Miles didn't want to embarrass Kyla any more than she already was. He'd never met a woman who blushed so easily at a compliment. "You know, Anthimos, I was thinking the same thing. She's a natural beauty."

Kyla threw her hands up. "Okay, thank you, but now I feel like a horse."

Everyone laughed. "Oh, no, that was not my intention. I just wanted the young man to know how lucky he was to be dining with such a beautiful young lady. I'm going to go back into my kitchen and let you two finish your lunch." Anthimos gave Kyla another hug. "We'll see you again in a few days. Tell everyone at the house I said hello."

Miles sat down as Anthimos turned to him. "Enjoy your stay, and come again. We're open for lunch every day."

"I will, thank you."

Kyla sat down, shaking her head as Anthimos walked away. "That man is something else. He's as sweet as he can be, and a big flirt."

"I think he likes you," Miles commented.

Kyla shook her head. "You have to know Anthimos. Every woman is the prettiest woman in town to him. He and his wife have no daughters and two sons. They help him run the restaurant, and neither one is married. I think he's trying to find a wife for one of them."

Miles laughed. "So he's trying to set you up with his son?"

She turned her lip up and shook her head. "He tried. It didn't work. Not my type."

"So, what is Kyla's type?" Miles asked.

She looked him up and down for a moment before looking away. From the way she twisted her lips, he thought maybe she'd answer him, but she abruptly changed her mind.

"No time for all that. We need to get back. Are you finished eating?" she asked.

"Yeah, I'm finished."

And so is this conversation, I guess. Unfortunate.

Chapter 8

Tuesday morning Kyla had to drag herself out of bed. The night before, she hadn't been able to focus on her studies because she had Miles on the brain. She even stopped and Googled him once more, but this time she read the articles about his hookups and breakups with a renewed interest. One article suggested that some of his hookups had been fabricated for publicity.

All morning she thought about why he would want or need to do that. She was still thinking about Miles when the truck ride was over and she was helping Tayler before her workshop.

She followed Tayler out onto the front porch with a pitcher of water for the plants.

"So, you think this is a good idea, huh?" she asked.

"Oh, yeah!" Tayler stood on a stepladder to water the hanging ferns. "I think his presence may have lasting benefits for the B and B. Now, if we can just get him to do a commercial for us."

"Huh! I don't know about that," Kyla said.

A gray Chrysler pulled up to the B and B, causing Kyla to squint and take a deep breath.

Tayler stopped watering the plants and held her hand up to shield the sun. "Who is that? We're full, so I'm not expecting anyone."

A tall, handsome young man in dark shades climbed out of the car with a big smile on his face. A smile that Kyla hadn't necessarily wanted to ever see again. "It's Don."

"Oh, yeah, I was going to ask you about him."

He walked up the steps. "Good morning, beautiful ladies. How's everything on this bright, sunshiny day?"

"Hey, Don." Kyla hoped the lack of enthusiasm in her voice revealed her level of excitement.

"Hello, Don. We haven't seen you in a while," Tayler said.

"Yes, ma'am. I've been working over in Mt. Sterling. I ran into an old friend at the grocery store who told me Kyla was working full-time for the summer. So I thought I'd stop by and say hello." He never took his eyes off Kyla as he talked.

Tayler climbed down off the stepladder. "Well, I've got some rooms to clean, so I'll leave you two to talk."

"It was nice seeing you again, Mrs. Coleman."

"It was nice seeing you, too, Don."

Kyla wasn't about to fall for Don's sweet guy routine. He was a jerk.

"What do you want Don?" she asked.

"Like I said, it's been a while, so I thought I'd stop by and say hello. You know, see how you're doing since you stopped returning my calls."

She crossed her arms. "I'm doing fine."

He gave her one of his *don't you think I'm sexy* smiles. In return, she gave him one of her *I'm not impressed with you* looks.

"I can see that." He paused to lick his lower lip. "Girl, you always look good. So, you're hanging out here for the whole summer?"

"I'm *working* here all summer, yes."

"Like, you moved out of student housing and everything?" He walked over to one of the rocking chairs and sat down.

"It was a graduate apartment, and yes, I moved out." She followed him with her eyes but not her body.

"That's cool. You know I finished my master's and accepted an occupational therapist position over at Ephraim Medical Center." He started rocking back and forth.

"No, I didn't know that. Congratulations."

"Thank you. That's probably because you didn't return my call. I thought we had a good time. What happened?"

Kyla didn't want one of the guests to walk out in the middle of their conversation, so she motioned for Don to follow her. "Come on. Let's take this out to your car."

He stood up. "Sorry. I forget this is like a hotel." He followed her down the steps.

The last time Kyla and Don went out she'd sworn would be the last. After a couple of dates he'd started smothering her. What little time she had for herself, he wanted it all spent with him. They went to the movies, out to eat, the typical small-town dates.

Truthfully, she'd found him—and the dates—boring.

Once they reached his car he turned around, facing her with his back against it. "So why'd I get the cold shoulder?"

She crossed her arms. "The last time we went out you were a little...how do I say this?"

"Assertive. Pushy. Maybe overly aggressive." He reached out and grabbed her by the elbows. "Kyla, when I want something, I go after it."

"That's the problem Don. I'm not something. I'm somebody. I needed room to breathe. Relationships should start off as friendships."

He let go of her and crossed his arms. "I thought we were friends."

Kyla shook her head and knew Don would never understand.

"How about we start over? I'm living here now, and you're not driving back and forth from Lexington. Somebody's trying to tell us something, don't you think?"

Kyla remembered explaining her program to him. He said it was cute and asked how that would help her get her degree. She chuckled at the thought. "Don, I'm sorry, but I have to go. My next workshop starts in a few minutes."

He pushed away from the car and reached out for her hands. "So, how about I call you in a couple of days and we can catch a movie or something?"

She kept backing up. "Sure."

He released her hands, winked and gave her the gun fingers. God, how she hated that.

"I'll see you soon."

From her peripheral vision she could see a few guests headed down the path to her workshop. She waved at Don as he pulled off. When she turned around, Miles was standing on the front porch talking on his cell phone. He waved at her.

She waved back and then headed to her workshop.

How much of that had he seen?

Miles stood on the porch talking to Glenda as he watched the guy in the Chrysler slowly moving down the driveway and Kyla heading toward the gazebo. She didn't look back once. For some reason, that gave Miles a glint of satisfaction. If the guy meant something to her, she'd at least have given him one more glance.

"Have they turned you into a farmer yet?" Glenda asked

through the phone, interrupting his concentrated focus on Kyla.

"Not yet, but she's working on it." He stepped off the porch and waved at the Nelsons, who were getting into their car. The Chrysler disappeared from sight down the long driveway.

"If you can tear yourself away later, maybe you can ride up to Nicholasville to see that piece of property I was telling you about. It's headed into foreclosure. I've emailed you all the information."

Miles walked down the path toward the gazebo. "Glenda, I'm not sure I'll be able to get away today."

"Miles, you've been down there for two days now. What would it hurt to slip away? I've already seen the property and it's perfect. I also contacted Dave Johnson, our real estate investor."

He tried to focus on Glenda, but couldn't get Kyla out of his mind. Maybe the guy in the Chrysler was her boyfriend? The subject of dating hadn't come up in their conversations so far.

"By the way," Glenda said, "I took Brandon with me and explained the negotiating details of buying foreclosed property. He already knew a lot. He's a smart kid."

"Of course he is. He's a Parker."

"Okay, I'm going to let you have that one."

Miles approached the gazebo where Kyla was poised and ready to transform into teacher mode—and he was ready to learn. When she glanced up at him, the corners of his mouth involuntarily turned up. "Hey, I gotta run," he said to Glenda. "I'll make it up there before the week's out, promise. I'll call you back with a full report."

"Thank you, Miles."

He hung up and placed his phone back in his pocket. Glenda didn't need to know the challenges he faced—like rethinking the vow of celibacy he'd made after spending only two days with Kyla.

* * *

Miles sat in the passenger seat of the truck with his elbow resting on the inside ledge of the door, as Kyla drove down a quiet backroad to Shiloh Baptist Church. He'd helped fill the truck bed with baskets of fruits and vegetables, and offered to help Kyla deliver them. She'd almost said no, thank you, due to the close confines of the truck, but Miles, with his firm thighs and strong arms, would be helpful. Besides, he was only interested in her program—not her.

"So, you make this run every Wednesday evening?" Miles asked.

Kyla took a deep breath to get her head right. She tried to look at Miles as if he were any other guy she'd met, but that was hard. "Yep, me or Kevin, but usually me."

"Is this part of Rooted Beginnings?"

She shook her head. "No, it's part of being a good Christian. The church gives out free food to those in need, so we try to add a little variety to the meals—some vegetables and fruits to balance out a good diet."

He nodded. "Wow, that's nice."

"I guess you can say it's a part of Rollin's tithing to the church. He's a big supporter of giving back. When he started the B and B, a lot of church members helped him—some even worked for free. And when he started selling at the farmers market, the members came out in mass support. This is Rollin's way of saying thank you."

"That's cool. Rollin's a good dude."

"I'll tell you something that is a part of Rooted Beginnings that you can help me with."

"Sure, what's that?"

"On Friday, I'll be spending a couple of hours visiting a local elementary school's summer food program. It's an interactive miniworkshop that, for me, is the heart of my program. I love working with kids, and I could use a helper. I think you'll enjoy yourself."

"That's cool. I wanted to see what you do with the school system, so thank you for the invite."

She shrugged. "You're welcome. You know, after we leave the church we've got some time before I have to be back for my afternoon workshop, so I was thinking about something. Do you remember my presentation at World Hunger Day, when I mentioned my friend's natural post-harvest protection project? It prolongs the life of organic vegetables."

He glanced over at her. "Yeah, I remember, and I wanted to ask you more about that."

"Well, he doesn't live far from here, and you did say you were open to new concepts in farming. So, if you're interested, I'd like to introduce you guys. I'm trying to help them get exposure. It's a wonderful project. If you're game, we can stop by their farm."

"Sure, I'm game."

"Great. It might be just the thing you're looking for."

"Who says I'm looking for something?"

She shrugged. "You're here, but your business has nothing to do with organic produce. You're searching for something." Somehow she figured it was more than just a learning experience.

"I'm seeking knowledge from the queen of organics," he proclaimed.

She laughed. *Uh-huh, sure you are.*

After a minute of silence, she asked, "Didn't you say your father was a minister?"

"Not a minister, but a missionary. He was a member of United Missionary Baptist Church in Atlanta. My whole family goes there."

"Do you go home often?" she asked, as she honked and waved at a passing motorist.

"A couple of times a year. I spent Mother's Day there a few weeks ago. It's always good to go home."

She agreed with him, which made her feel guiltier about the last time she was home. "With the work you do, I'm surprised you didn't go the same route as your father."

Miles laughed. "Me, a missionary! I'm afraid I went in the opposite direction as soon as I finished high school. There's no other man like my pops. He was one in a million."

"Did he ever see you play professionally?" she asked as they arrived at Shiloh and she pulled into the parking lot.

"Yes, he did. Many times."

"You're blessed," she said.

"That I am."

She backed the truck into a parking space close to the back door. Several vehicles were scattered around the lot, a few of which Kyla expected. She had dreaded riding alone with Miles, but after their conversation she couldn't remember why. He sounded like a solid guy with a good head on his shoulders. She'd enjoyed his company.

He grabbed the baskets from the truck bed, displaying his muscular strength, as if they weighed an ounce. She was grateful for the help and happy for the view. He followed her through an unlocked back door down the hall to the kitchen. Kyla showed him where to leave the food, and they walked out. When they reached the church's atrium, the sound of female voices filled the air.

"Are they having bible study?" Miles asked.

"No, it's The Color of Success. Tayler and Corra run a nonprofit empowerment group for young women. The program holds workshops here every Wednesday evening for girls in the community," Kyla said as they reached the classroom and she peeked in.

Miles stopped beside her. His voice lowered, he asked, "Exactly what do they do?"

Several heads were turned around, peeking back at them. "She teaches them how to be young ladies and how to succeed in life," Kyla whispered, as Tayler motioned them in.

Miles glanced down at his dirty shorts and T-shirt before giving Kyla an apologetic look. They'd been out working in the garden most of the morning and seeding after lunch. This ride to the church was the first real break Miles had taken all day, and he still looked handsome.

"Don't worry about it, they're kids. I doubt they know who you are." Kyla shrugged, hoping to make him feel better. Miles slowly walked into the room.

Tayler started introducing Miles before he reached the front of the room, and once there, she asked him to tell a quick story about what it took to make it to the major leagues. He was exactly the type of successful person Tayler wanted to parade before the girls.

Corra joined Kyla, giving her a quick hug. "I'm so glad you guys stopped by when you did. What a wonderful opportunity for the girls."

Kyla smiled, knowing that Miles would be a hit. "Yeah, I just hope he doesn't mind. We've been working really hard, so I know he wasn't prepared for this."

Corra crossed her arms. "I'm sure he doesn't mind. I can't believe we didn't think to invite him. If Tayler had asked, I'm certain he would have said yes. He's such a nice guy."

Miles was a natural orator. He spoke to the girls as if he'd already had something prepared. Kyla liked his display of confidence and how he seemed at ease in any situation.

"So, what's it like having a celebrity shadow your every move?" Corra asked.

Kyla turned and whispered in Corra's ear, "Nerve-racking."

As promised, once their stop in the workshop was finished, she swung by her friend Rorie's small farm and introduced Miles to his natural postharvest protection project. The two men had a lot to talk about and Miles seemed genuinely interested, which made Kyla happy.

Miles was going to leave there with more than an education, if she had anything to do with it.

Chapter 9

Kyla heard sounds of excitement coming from outside as she walked down the hall toward the back door. It was Thursday afternoon, and several of the guests were out enjoying the town or participating in whatever event had brought them to Danville. However, she was surprised when she opened the back door and saw Miles among the crowd of people scattered about the yard.

"Okay Jamie, remember what I told you about raising your heels. Only the balls of your feet and toes should be in contact with the ground," Miles instructed as he prepared to toss the ball to Corra's son.

She'd happened onto what appeared to be a family baseball game at four in the afternoon. She walked over to join Corra and Tayler, who were sitting in lounge chairs under a big oak tree next to the house. Scattered around a makeshift baseball diamond in the backyard were Corra's kids, Jamie and Katie, along with Kevin, Ben, Sean and one of the guests with her young son.

"Kyla, pull up a chair and relax a few minutes," Tayler suggested.

"Who started this impromptu game?" Kyla asked, as she walked over and confiscated a chair from the flowerbed area.

"I told Chris about Miles, and he had Jamie up all evening talking about how good of a baseball player he was," Corra said. "When I picked him up from school he practically begged me to bring him out here. Girl, I think he slept with that damned glove, he was so excited."

"It's nice of Miles to take the time to give him some pointers. He's a really nice guy, isn't he?" Tayler directed her question to Kyla.

Kyla nodded in agreement before sitting down and turning her attention back to the game. She watched them play for about thirty minutes, noting how Miles took the time to explain and demonstrate everything to Jamie and the others. The kids' faces were lit up like Christmas trees.

Kyla smiled as she watched Miles do his thing. This reminded her of yesterday at the church when he spoke to the Color of Success group. He'd had those little girls eating out of his hands with the story of how he worked his way onto a professional baseball team. There was something about a man displaying his nurturing, softer side that turned her on. Maybe Miles was right, and he wasn't all about chasing women.

After the impromptu ballgame, everyone cleaned up and prepared for dinner. As usual, the family ate in the kitchen after the guests were served. The baseball game was the topic of conversation.

"Kyla, maybe you can ask Miles for a picture of him playing baseball to—"

"No!" Kyla cut Tracee off. "I'm not about to ask him for

another picture. He checked in under an assumed name. He doesn't want the publicity."

"That's right, Tracee, we can't put upon him again," Tayler added, clearing her throat. "Besides, he's here to spend time with Kyla. It was nice enough that he spoke to the girls on Wednesday evening, but we shouldn't exploit the man."

Kyla glanced over at Tayler, who winked at her.

Corra's chin jutted out. "If anybody's being exploited, it's Kyla. He's taking up all her time. She hasn't been able to help me in the gift shop once since he's been here."

Kyla angled her body away from Corra, who was sitting next to her. "Corra, I didn't know you needed my help. You never said anything."

Corra gave a half-hearted shrug. "Well, it's not every day that we have such a high-profile customer, so I've been managing, but I miss you popping in and helping out."

"Oh, for the love of God." Rollin smiled and tossed his napkin on the table. "Ladies, Miles is an entrepreneur and a philanthropist who partners with other nonprofits all the time. He's here specifically to check out Kyla's program, so let's let him do that."

"Oh, he's checking out something, all right. But I'm not sure it's her program," Tracee speculated.

"There you go, Tracee," Kyla uttered. "Your mind's in the gutter again. You think every man is after one thing."

Suddenly, all the women at the table were talking over each other as they discussed Miles's interest in Kyla. She caught Rollin's attention. He shrugged and gave her a helpless smile. She shook her head and lowered her chin into her chest. Her love life always seemed to be a topic of conversation. She'd had enough.

"You guys are too much," she said, picking up her empty dinner plate and walking over to put it in the dishwasher.

Rollin stood at the same time. "Okay, ladies, that's enough. Who wants to go for a bike ride? The bikes are fixed and waiting out back."

A loud scuffling noise came from the card table where the children sat. Jamie and Katie hurried from the table out the back door. Corra called after them. "You guys had better not disappear on those bikes! We have to go. Chris will be home any minute now."

Kyla laughed because those kids didn't even slow down. "I'll make sure they don't go anywhere," she said as she walked out after them. Anything to get away from these women who, no doubt, were plotting her future with Miles.

In the backyard, the kids were circling the bikes, trying to select the ones they wanted to ride. A bike path ran along the back of the house, past the vegetable fields, down to a creek several miles away.

"Whoa! What do we have here?"

Kyla turned around to see Miles walking her way. He'd changed into another pair of cargo shorts and a T-shirt displaying his company logo. Despite all the work they'd done that day, he looked relaxed, refreshed and extremely handsome.

The kids gravitated to him like bees to a wildflower. You would have thought he was the ice-cream man. She didn't have to explain a thing as the kids filled him in on the bicycles that were provided for guests. Each one grabbed a bike and started to climb on.

The back door swung open. "What did I tell y'all?" Corra called out in a firm, hushed voice as she descended the stairs. "You can come back and ride this weekend. Right now we have to go home." Corra joined them, all five congregating around the bikes.

"Miles, I'm glad I bumped into you before we left. Chris is still expecting you and Rollin out at the house later this evening," she said before glancing at Kyla. "That is, if you don't have other plans?"

Kyla quickly shook her head. How many times did she have to tell them this man was not there for her? Once their work was done for the day, he was free to do whatever he liked.

Miles smiled. "I guess I'll be there. Tell him I'm looking forward to it," Miles said.

Corra smiled. "Great, then we'll see you later." She gave Kyla a hug and whispered in her ear, "Enjoy him while you can." Then she rounded up the kids and headed for her car.

"So, these are for anybody?" Miles asked, taking a silver bike off the rack.

"They are. We have a bike path that runs down by Miller's Creek."

Miles positioned himself on the bike and rode around in a little circle. "Man, I can't remember the last time I was on a bicycle. At least, one that wasn't stationary." He stopped the bike next to Kyla.

She held out her hand, thinking he was a little too close and might ride over her foot.

"I bet you don't even know how to ride a bike, do you?" he asked.

She crossed her arms. "Of course I know how to ride a bicycle. I grew up in the country, remember?"

"Somehow I don't see Ms. Kyla leisurely riding around on a bicycle. Prove to me you know how to ride." He kept the bike in motion, continuing to circle her.

The nerve of him challenging her to ride a bike. Did he think she was so academic that she didn't know how to have fun? "I don't have to prove anything to you."

"Yeah, just what I thought. You can't ride. Besides, it would be too much like having fun." He grinned and kept circling.

Kyla surprised even herself when she walked over,

jumped onto a red bike and took off down the path. Before dinner, she'd showered and changed out of her work uniform into a pair of stretchy jeans and her favorite T-shirt that read Runs on Veggies. On her feet were a pair of flip-flops. Not exactly bike riding gear, but she couldn't resist his challenge.

"Oh! Okay, I see you Ms. Kyla. You can ride!" Miles announced as he turned his bike in her direction and followed her.

Miles hadn't expected Kyla to jump on a bike and take off. For the last couple of days, he'd wanted to see the fun side of her. Maybe today she was ready to show it to him. He pedaled faster to catch up with her.

The bike path was flanked with large trees, which should have shielded them from the summer heat. However, it was late and the sun was setting. He slowed down to pedal alongside her.

"I don't know what made you think I wouldn't know how to ride a bike," she said, smiling at him for the first time that day.

"Maybe because it's hard to see you having fun. You're a pretty serious woman, Ms. Kyla."

"Just Kyla, please. It's not like I'm your elder or anything." She smiled, throwing his previously used words back at him, and then she pumped faster, moving ahead.

Miles liked her sassy attitude. He liked it a lot. "Okay, Kyla."

He continued to follow her down the path, enjoying the views—both around him and the luscious one moving as one with the bike ahead of him. He needed to move his focus from her body if he was going to make it through the rest of the week. In the quiet of this path, with Kyla only a few feet away, he could now admit to himself that he was attracted to her.

Being celibate for the past year had helped his business and done wonders for his focus. Fewer distractions of the female kind had made him a better businessman. But this decision to spend a week close to Kyla Coleman no longer had anything to do with business. He wasn't sure when things had changed, but he was experiencing pure, selfish lust, and he had to face up to that—and the consequences.

After several minutes of steady riding, Kyla's bike slowed down, allowing Miles to pull up next to her.

"Are you having fun yet?" she asked.

"I am. What better way to unwind after a long day on the farm?"

Kyla laughed. "You sound like you've been working on a farm for years. What's it been? Four days now?"

"Four really long days, I might add. But I don't mind, because I've had the opportunity to spend them in the company of a very beautiful woman."

Kyla glanced behind her to insinuate he was talking about someone else.

He laughed. "Yeah, I'm talking about you. Kyla Coleman. Accept it."

She bit her bottom lip and blushed.

They rode along for a few minutes in silence. The path cleared on the left side, opening to the vegetable fields and revealing a beautiful sunset on the horizon. The farm looked larger from the seat of a bicycle.

"We're about halfway to the creek now," she informed him.

"How big is the farm, anyway?" he asked, concerned about making it to the creek and back before dark.

"About thirty acres. But the creek's not that far. Let's see how much of it we can cover before we have to head back." She picked up speed, taking off again.

"Oh, you want to race, I see." Miles stood up on his

bike to pick up speed. He sped past Kyla and continued down the path.

"It's supposed to be a leisurely ride!" she called out.

"You're the one who wants to race!" he yelled back. Within minutes they were under the cover of large trees again. Miles looked back over his shoulder to see Kyla hot on his heels. The big smile of joy on her face was one he hadn't seen before. Her ponytail swung in the wind behind her, and he knew he was falling for this woman...maybe harder than he had for any other woman.

For the first time in a long time, Miles grinned from ear to ear for no reason as the wind whipped across his face and body. The last time he'd gone cycling with a girl, he'd been in junior high. He glanced back over his shoulder again, and Kyla was right behind him.

"Relaxing isn't it?" he yelled as he pedaled harder to pull away from her.

He heard Kyla's laugh—right before he heard her scream.

Chapter 10

Miles jerked his head around in time to see Kyla's bike pitch right, sending her flying over the handlebars. A flush of adrenaline ran through his body. He slammed on his brakes and jumped off the bike. He ran back to Kyla, lying in the gravel, moaning in pain.

"Don't move." He squatted next to her and ran his hands along the back of her head and neck.

"Oh, my God! That hurt!"

"Did you hit your head?"

She shook her head. "I don't think so. Ouch! But my arm," she grunted.

Miles helped her sit up before holding up her arm and seeing blood dripping from her elbow. She pulled her arm back and winced in pain. She twisted her arm around for a better view.

"Aww, man, look at that," Kyla said before checking the other arm.

"Can you stand up?" he asked.

She took a deep breath. "I think so."

He held her by the other elbow and helped her up. "What, we weren't going fast enough for you, so you decided to try to fly?" he asked, attempting to keep his voice light.

Kyla bent over, trying to stifle a laugh. "Don't make me laugh, it hurts."

Miles looked down at her flip-flops. "I see what happened," he said, pointing to her feet. "Your foot must have slipped, then you landed on a sharp rock."

One flip-flop had flown off in the fall. She stepped lightly over and slipped it back on. "I hit something and I tried to stop, but when I hit the brake my foot slipped off the pedal." Still holding her arms out, with the blood oozing from her wound and now dripping to the ground, she searched herself for any other wounds.

Miles walked over to her, pulling his T-shirt over his head as he moved. He folded the material and held it against her bloody arm. "This should stop the bleeding. Are you hurt anywhere else?"

She hesitated before reaching across her body to rub her side. "I think I skinned my hip, too."

Against his better judgment, he raised her elbow up. "Let me see."

With her opposite hand, she grabbed her T-shirt on the side of her injured elbow and pulled it up. For a nanosecond, Miles stared transfixed at the sight of her smooth brown skin. Then he slid a thumb into the waistband of her jeans, carefully pulling the fabric away and then down a little. She winced and sucked in a breath. Miles held his breath, too, as he inspected the oasis of lovely skin.

"It's sore," she said.

"But the skin isn't broken," he added with relief.

Miles wanted to place his hand next to hers, caressing the spot to make it feel better. Instead, she dropped her T-shirt, and he lowered her elbow. He gently removed his T-shirt to see that she was still bleeding, so he repositioned the shirt.

"I'm sorry about this," she said.

He shook his head. "It's not your fault, it's mine. I shouldn't have challenged you in the first place. Then I should have slowed down. Like you said, this was supposed to be a leisurely ride."

"Well, no harm. I think I'll live." She cradled her arm against her side.

"Here, let me tie this up for you." He rewrapped his T-shirt around her elbow and tied it so neither of them would have to hold it. He hoped she couldn't feel the slight tremble in his hands as he touched her. That's when he realized she was staring at his bare chest.

"How did you do that?" she asked.

His heart raced as her hand reached out for his chest. He looked down at the jagged scar across the right side of his chest as she brushed it with her fingertips. *No, don't do that!* He took a deep breath. "I, uh…fell off a motorcycle in high school and landed on a piece of glass."

She nodded and slowly stared her way up his chest to his eyes. He could hear his heartbeat pounding in his ears.

"Did you have to get stitches?" she asked in a soft voice.

He bit his bottom lip, unable to speak. He only nodded. The sweet scent of her skin was like a magnet, pulling him toward her. Her lips were plump and ripe for kissing. He couldn't wait to taste her; he knew it was coming, and it would be, oh, so sweet. His heart raced as he leaned forward—

Just as she lowered her head and examined the shirt around her elbow. "Thank you. But I'm afraid you'll be mosquito food if we go anywhere near the creek."

He ran a hand behind his neck and squeezed. *What the hell am I doing?* He'd wanted to kiss her, but he knew he shouldn't. Why was he torturing himself like this? He turned his head and looked up toward the darkening sky. "Yeah, maybe we'd better head back." He let out a deep breath as he walked over and picked up her bike. He immediately noticed the chain had come off.

"You wouldn't happen to have a wrench in your pocket, would you?" he asked, as he knelt down next to the wheels.

"No, I don't. You can't just pop it back on?" she asked.

"Afraid not." He fiddled with the wheel to see if he could get it off with his hands, with no luck.

She squatted next to him. "I'm so sorry. I should have been watching where I was going."

Miles let go of the bike and wiped his hands on his pants. At the moment, Kyla was talking fast and more than she had since he'd been there. She sounded nervous as she rattled on, apologizing again and again. He couldn't hold back any longer, so he leaned into her, getting her instant attention. She stopped talking. Miles placed his hand against the back of her head, pulling her closer to him. And kissed her.

Her lips were soft and her breath warm. Her body froze at his touch. She didn't pull away, so he closed his eyes and kissed her again, this time running his tongue across her lips. He'd never been surer than he was right now that he wanted this woman. Her mouth opened a little and her body loosened. Greedily, he went for the gusto and dropped to his knees while reaching out with his other hand to steady her face. He kissed her like a man who'd been celibate for over a year. Too much, too fast.

Kyla placed a hand against Miles's chest and pushed back. He released her head and she fell backwards, flat onto her butt.

"Damn! I'm sorry," he said as he quickly stood up, pulling her with him.

She looked flushed as she accepted his hand. He reached down to help brush the dirt from her butt.

"That's okay," she said, taking a step back. "They're just some old jeans."

"Kyla, I didn't... I mean... What I'm trying to say is, I didn't mean to do that. Well, I did, but not *like* that." He stumbled over his words, trying to find a tactful way to apologize. He'd embarrassed himself.

He took a deep breath. "Okay, I didn't mean to let you fall, but I did mean to kiss you. Although I should be staying away from you, instead."

She was still staring at his chest, heating his body up from the inside out on this seventy-degree evening.

"Kyla?" Miles took a step back and tilted his head as he grinned at her. "You okay?"

She grabbed her elbow and frowned. "I'm fine. I'm just trying to figure out what made you think it was okay to kiss me."

"I don't know. Maybe because you kissed me back!" He took a step back and ran a hand across his face. "I don't have to tell you that I find you very attractive. I'm sure you picked that up over the last few days. And I thought I felt something coming from you, too, but I may have been wrong. Anyway, I apologize." He walked over and picked up the bike, busted chain and all.

"Apology accepted," she replied from behind him.

"Well, I think we need to head back. But this bike's not going anywhere. I'll leave it here and come back for it tomorrow. The walk back's going to be much longer than the fast ride down here." He set her bike against some bushes and went to pick up his.

"Want to ride back on the handlebars?" he asked, holding the bike steady.

She held her T-shirt-wrapped arm up. "No way! The last thing I need is to fall off again. I'll walk."

He looked up at the evening sky. "Don't happen to know any shortcuts to get us back to the house, do you?" he asked.

She shook her head.

As they walked back along the gravel path, Miles asked Kyla what to expect tomorrow during the school visit. She gave him a brief overview of the day. Then she stopped and asked him something he hadn't expected.

"Miles, what did you mean when you said you should be staying away from me?"

He lowered his gaze and took a deep breath. He shook his head, gazing at Kyla. "Let's keep walking. I'll explain."

The sun had disappeared and twilight was upon them. Miles knew they would be engulfed in darkness pretty soon.

"A couple of days ago we talked about the pretty fast life I used to live. I made a lot of money and had a good time spending it. I went through cash and women in a fashion that would not have made my father proud. One day, I looked in the mirror and I realized I wasn't the man my father raised. Nor was I the man I wanted my little brother to emulate. It was time to do something about that. So I decided I had to slow down." He cleared his throat. "I prayed about it before deciding to…well…take a vow of celibacy."

Kyla pursed her lips and tilted her head slightly. "I'm sorry. I don't mean to disrespect your vow or anything, but earlier this week when you spoke about media perception, I thought you were saying you never lived that life."

He nodded and kept walking. "I *used* to live that life. Those days are long gone."

He glanced over at her and could see the puzzlement on her face. He hadn't told many women about his vow for that exact reason. He really wanted to know what was going through her mind right now.

"So…how long has it been?"

"A little over a year now. Thirteen months, to be exact."

"Wow, that's so long," she said. "It takes a strong man to do that. I commend you."

He chuckled. "Thank you." He'd been strong until tonight.

As twilight turned into night, they finally reached the beginning of the path at the end of the backyard. Kyla let out a deep breath. All the lights in the house were on.

"Well, I'm sure we're going to have some explaining to do," Miles said before he walked the bike up to the rack and placed it in. He swatted at his skin as another mosquito took a bite into his flesh.

Kyla unwrapped his T-shirt from her elbow, which was still bleeding. "I was going to give you this back, but I think I'd better keep it on. I'll wash it and give it back to you tomorrow."

"Not a problem. But you do need to clean that gash up."

The back door opened and Tayler stepped out. "Hey! What happened to you guys? I thought we were going to have to come looking for you." She hurried down the steps. The minute she noticed Miles didn't have a shirt on, and then saw it wrapped around Kyla's arm, she stopped. "Oh, my goodness! What happened?"

Miles spoke up. "I'm afraid we had an accident. Kyla cut her arm, and we busted the chain on one of the bikes. That's what took so long—we walked back."

"We didn't bust the chain—I did," Kyla confessed.

"Well, let's get in here and take a look at that arm. How bad is the cut?" Tayler asked, walking over to inspect the bloody T-shirt. "Oh, Miles. Rollin's waiting for you. He said Chris is expecting you guys this evening."

"Right. Tell him I'm going to jump in the shower and I'll be ready in a few minutes." Then he turned to Kyla. "Take care of that arm, and let me know if you need anything. Otherwise, I'll see you first thing in the morning, cool?"

"Bright and early," she replied, with a half smile.

Miles hurried around to the front of the house, thinking about what a fool he'd made of himself out there. It wasn't too often that he misjudged a woman—and he still didn't think he'd misjudged Kyla.

Tayler helped Kyla clean up the gash in her arm. Then Kayla went to her room, stripped off her T-shirt and slacks and slipped on an oversized nightshirt.

In order to unwind, she turned on the television and sat on the edge of the bed. She wasn't even watching the program because she had one thing on her mind. Miles Parker had kissed her! Instead of enjoying the moment, she'd questioned him about it.

She'd had a déjà vu moment, only Miles wasn't the guy kissing her, it was Louis. Her first boyfriend and the guy she'd thought was the one. Cool and confident, Louis had been the star of the basketball team and the guy every girl in school wanted to date. He and Kyla were inseparable throughout the eleventh grade. They'd taken long bike rides together during summer break. Louis had been the first boy Kyla let kiss her. But the first week of their senior year, Louis met a cheerleader and ended their relationship. The hurt and humiliation had stayed with her long after high school. Now the memory reared its ugly little head and made her suspicious of every man she met.

A knock at the door grabbed Kyla's attention. She sat straight up in bed.

"Kyla?" Tayler's voice came from the other side of the door.

She jumped off the bed. "Yeah, just a minute." She walked over to open the door.

With her arms crossed and her head tilted to the side, Tayler smiled at Kyla. "So, how was your ride with Miles? Aside from the fall?"

Kyla shifted from one foot to the other, about to burst from wanting to tell Tayler what had happened tonight. If anybody could keep it to themselves, Tayler could. "It was cool. I think he had a good time."

"How about you? Did you enjoy yourself?"

Did I! Kyla bit the inside of her mouth to keep her face from exploding with joy. "It was nice. I hadn't been on a bike in a long time."

Tayler took a deep breath. "It is fun. Rollin and I used to go riding after we purchased them. It can be romantic, too," she added with a raised brow.

"Unless it ends like this," Kyla said, holding up her arm.

Tayler smiled big. "Yeah, well, I don't mean to pry, I was just thinking—"

"He kissed me!" Kyla blurted out. She pressed her lips together, anxious to see Tayler's reaction.

Tayler's mouth fell open before she glanced up and down the hall with wide eyes. Then she hurried into Kyla's room and closed the door behind her. "You're kidding!"

Overcome with giddiness, Kyla shook her head and began fanning herself. Then she started at the beginning and told Tayler everything.

Chapter 11

Every Friday, Rooted Beginnings participated in the Summer Food Program, assisting with teaching children eligible for free and reduced-price lunches about healthy eating.

Miles joined Kyla today, which impressed the program volunteers as well as Mrs. Snowden, the school principal. The conversation between Kyla and Miles so far had been brief. After that kiss on the trail yesterday, she was careful about getting too close or touching him. She hadn't fallen asleep until well into the early hours of the morning, unable to get Miles off her mind. She'd been up when he and Rollin returned from Corra's house, and she wanted to hear all about the visit. Eventually, Corra would tell her.

Kyla started the day's program with a brief PowerPoint presentation, displaying the three key facts about food: all food comes from plants or animals; food has to be farmed, caught or grown at home; and food is changed from farm to fork. After that, she threw in a few interactive exercises to keep the kids interested.

"Where does my food come from?" Kyla asked the group of kids, who were mixed ages from several Glenn County elementary schools.

A few looked lost, but most of the twenty or so kids screamed out, "The farm!" Kyla pretended to be knocked over by their words, and Miles followed suit. Giggles and laughter circled the room.

Usually Kyla selected a volunteer to serve as her helper, but today Miles held that position. When she reached for a box of fruit she was going to use in the next exercise, Miles leaned down and placed his hands over hers. Kyla jumped as she released the box.

"I'll get that. I'm your helper, remember," he said with a wink and a smile.

She took a step back and glanced around the room to see if any of the adults noticed her reaction. "Yeah, sure, just sit it on the desk in the back." She had a fluttery feeling in the pit of her stomach. After Miles placed the box in the back of the room, he leaned against the windowsill and crossed his arms, staring at her.

She heard the nervous quiver of her own voice. The way Miles looked at her had her thinking about his muscular chest and how he'd held her face in his hands to kiss her yesterday.

She forced herself to get back to the game before the kids took over the room.

They loved the games, but appeared to love Miles more. He'd emerged from the back of the room to walk around, helping a few of them, and in the middle of one game a little boy asked Miles, "Where's your baseball cap?"

When Miles cut his eyes at Kyla and shrugged, she encouraged him to answer their questions. She figured once the questions were out of the way, they could get back to learning where their food came from. Ten minutes later, Kyla had to cut the questions and exercises short and move on to the outside garden.

At the start of the program, she'd helped the class plant a small raised-bed vegetable garden behind the school. Today they were going to pick tomatoes and lettuce that would be consumed with their lunch. The kids practically tripped over each other running out to the garden. Some of the adult volunteers joined them, while Miles hung back talking to Principal Snowden. Before Kyla left the building, he joined her.

"Kyla, I have to tell you, today was more than I expected," Miles admitted.

Kyla turned around, but kept her arms crossed. "What were you expecting, cooking classes?" she asked with a smirk.

"Actually, yes. You said lunch was being served. But you have these kids excited about going to pick tomatoes."

She laughed. "Don't tell them, but at the end of the program I'm going to give each of them a pot of sugar snap peas to take home. They grow well in this July heat. Hopefully it will be the start of something big. How about you?" she asked.

His eyes widened. "How about me what?"

"After this week, are you ready to go home and plant some vegetables?"

Miles laughed and shook his head. "No disrespect. I love everything you're doing with your program. I'm just not that guy. It's been an enlightening experience, and it's not over yet." His voice lowered at the end of his sentence. He caressed her face with his eyes as a slow smile spread across his face.

Every time Kyla looked into his eyes, she felt like a schoolgirl who'd developed a crush on the boy who sat next to her in class. Under his intense stare, the hair on her arms rose. Something had happened to her yesterday, and she couldn't control her emotions today.

"Hey! Are you guys coming out?" One of the volunteers poked his head back inside the building.

Embarrassed, Kyla uncrossed her arms. "We're right behind you." She glanced up at Miles, seeing the beauty and charm that oozed out of him.

He held out his hand, gesturing ahead of him. "After you."

Outside, Kyla observed that in four short days Miles had learned something. He was a pro at helping the kids pick vegetables. When he caught her looking at him, he merely smiled, and she wanted to crawl under a table. Why couldn't she take her eyes off this man? Her attention needed to be focused on the kids.

Principal Snowden had joined them, helping a few of the rowdy boys pick vegetables. Kyla had worked her way down across from them.

"Kyla, we've never had a celebrity join the class before. Thank you so much for bringing him." Principal Snowden beamed up at Kyla.

"You're welcome." Kyla helped the little girl with her pick some lettuce.

"You know, I was surprised to learn that he's in the food services industry, as well," Principal Snowden said as she walked alongside Kyla.

"So was I," Kyla said. "He's very passionate about ending hunger in third-world countries."

Principal Snowden tilted her head. "Oh, I didn't know that. When we spoke, I got the impression he was more of a supplier. Like he could supply our program with all the seeds we need all year round."

Kyla blinked a few times more than normal. Principal Snowden gave her the oddest look.

"So he asked you about getting into the program?"

"Not exactly, but I don't see why it isn't something he could propose. Maybe you could help him, or give him some pointers on how you did it."

Kyla ran her tongue across her front teeth. Yeah, she could give him some pointers, all right. He wanted to spread his genetically modified seeds into her natural organic beds—no way. And why would he even suggest that when he knew it ran counter to her program? Instead of giving him any advice she wanted to ask him what he was up to by speaking to the principal about his business.

The minute Miles climbed into the truck he started sharing his experience with Kyla.

"Okay, that was more than I expected. One little girl wanted to tell me everything she knows about vegetables. It was cute actually. Then one little guy started telling me everything you can do with some lettuce. I mean, those kids are bright."

"Of course they are," Kyla added.

"One little dude even asked me my batting average. I was impressed. What grade did you say they were in?"

"Fifth and sixth," Kyla said. "The program is for children from low-income families. They sign up for these day camps to get good food that meets federal nutritional guidelines. For some, it may be the only nutritious meal they get all day."

"How did you learn about the program?"

"During the school year, I work with Principal Snowden. She found out about the program through the county system and asked if I would be a sponsor. I jumped at the chance. The more people I can reach, the better."

"But you're one woman. I don't know how you expect to feed or teach the masses all by yourself. Does your program have a teach-the-teacher component to it?"

Kyla smiled. "Yes, of course, which is how I plan to reach the masses. A couple of times a year I hold a week-long training workshop for teachers, community leaders or anyone who wants to learn the benefits of organic gardening and how sustainability works."

"I like the way you've partnered with the school system. Ms. Snowden said there are other food service projects all over the state."

"She mentioned you spoke to her. I hope you're not trying to sell them on genetically modified seeds. I thought you were more interested in third-world countries?"

"Oh, I was just talking to her hypothetically. Like I said before, we're a small company and I'm always open to new ideas. I've had some of the best food I've ever put in my mouth this week, and I've learned about the labor of love that goes into every meal. Guess you can say you've made a believer out of me. I can already tell that Rooted Beginnings is going to be a huge success. You're amazing, you know that? And watching your work with those kids…it was kind of sexy."

Kyla narrowed her eyes. "This week *has* been hard on you, hasn't it?"

Miles laughed. "No, really. I'm serious. Watching you work does something to me."

She rolled her eyes. "You've been digging in the dirt too long."

Miles turned in the passenger seat, facing her. "Thank you for allowing me to tag along to see you in another element."

Kyla glanced over at him, still a little skeptical. "Sure. I'm just doing my job."

When Kyla pulled up to the B and B, Don's car caught her eye. What did he want? She hadn't encouraged him or given him any indication that she was eager to see him again.

Standing on the front porch in a shirt and tie, with a

pair of black shades on, Don turned at the sound of an approaching car. He'd always been a handsome man who could have just about any woman in the county he wanted. So why was he back here?

Instead of pulling around back, she stopped short in the driveway.

"A friend of yours?" Miles asked, looking up at the house.

"An old friend, yes." She killed the engine of the truck. "I'll let you out up here. I hope you enjoyed the visit."

Miles turned to Kyla, and seemed to be studying her for a moment. "I enjoyed the visit and the company. All week, in fact. One more night and I'll be checking out."

"You're leaving tomorrow?" she asked.

"Yeah, tomorrow morning. I have a business to get back to. I'm meeting my business partner in Nicholasville for a meeting on the way back."

Her heart pounded in her chest. She had this evening with Miles, and that was it.

"Well—" he looked at his watch "—I think it's time for a lemonade break. We timed it just right—won't Mrs. Rita be setting refreshments out right about now?"

Kyla didn't even examine the clock in the truck. She just nodded.

"Looks like your friend is getting impatient," Miles said.

Kyla peeked around him to see Don slowly coming down the steps, holding his hand up to shield the sun. Miles opened the truck door and stepped out.

She finally climbed out and rounded the back end of the truck in time to see Miles reach out his hand and introduce himself. Don removed his shades, and recognition covered his face. She giggled inside—finally, someone more important than Don.

"Hey, what's up baby?" Don leaned over to give Kyla a kiss on the cheek.

She leaned back, staring at him as if he was crazy. He hadn't been in the habit of kissing her whenever he saw her. The screen door made a sound, and she looked up to see Miles looking back over his shoulder at them.

She took a step back. "What do you want, Don?"

He backed off. When he stared down at Kyla, she could see the jealousy in his face. But she wasn't sure why. It wasn't like they were dating.

Don crossed his arms. "I thought I'd come by to see if you still wanted to catch a movie or something tonight." Then he tilted his head toward the door. "But I see they've got you entertaining the celebrity guest."

"Can we talk out by your car? You forget this is a place of business." She walked out to the parking lot and Don followed her.

"Don, you haven't called me and I haven't agreed to date you. But you show up asking if I want to go out tonight? No, I don't. And you should have called first."

He shrugged. "Hey, I didn't have your number so I decided to try to catch you early. But if you—"

Kyla didn't hear another word he said. The screen door opened again and Miles, along with one of the other guests, stepped out onto the front porch. He sat in one of the big rockers on the porch and drank his lemonade while staring out at them.

"Don, I'm sorry but I'm just not interested in dating right now. I'm working on my PhD, you know."

He bit the inside of his cheek and nodded before glancing back up to the porch. "Yeah, I remember." He shook his head, dug in his pocket and found his car keys, staring down at them. "You know what your problem is?" he said, lowering his shades and looking over them.

She crossed her arms. "What's my problem, Don?"

"You don't know how to loosen up. Just because you're getting your PhD doesn't mean everything has to be so serious all the damn time. Give yourself permission to be spontaneous."

"By going to a movie with you?" she asked, thinking how ridiculous that sounded.

"Yes. Why should I have to call you days in advance to catch a movie? You want to control everything. Let your guard down a little, and let a man be a man."

She blinked several times, unable to believe the words coming out of his mouth. "A man makes plans for a date, he doesn't just swing by when he doesn't have anything better to do."

He sucked his teeth and shook his head, as if she didn't get it, when he was actually the one who didn't get it. "And for your information, I do spontaneous things all the time. I just won't be doing anything spontaneous tonight with you."

He walked around her and opened his car door. "Well, if you change your mind, you know where to find me." He climbed in the car, started the engine and pulled away.

Kyla couldn't believe he still wanted to take her out after what she'd just said to him. If Miles wasn't sitting on the porch, she'd have told him off. However, she didn't want Miles to overhear her conversation. She walked up the steps and noticed Miles was alone on the porch now.

"Got a hot date tonight?" he asked.

"No, I don't," she replied in as pleasant a tone as she could muster up, and reached for the doorknob.

He set his glass on the side table and motioned toward the parking lot. "Was that your boyfriend?"

She shook her head. "No."

"Don't go in. Why don't you sit out here and enjoy the breeze with me for a minutes. Take your mind off things."

She took a deep breath and relaxed her tensed up shoulders. Could Miles have heard her conversation?

"Come on, five minutes. Keep me company." He pointed to the other rocker on the porch.

Kyla decided to give him a few minutes. She walked away from the door and eased down into the rocker taking another deep breath.

"See there, don't you feel better already?"

She glanced over at the big smile on his face. "I guess it's a nice way to wind down before I go in and hit the books." She sit back and closed her eyes. "You've got five minutes."

Chapter 12

Kyla cut and pasted information from one paragraph to another. No matter what she typed, nothing sounded right. She typed and erased, over and over again, until she gave up and turned off her computer. It was no use—she couldn't get Miles off her brain. The look he'd given her when he asked if Don was her boyfriend totally surprised her. He looked a little curious, hopeful and jealous, all rolled into one expression. She shook her head, thinking that couldn't be the case.

She sat back and ran her fingers across her lips, thinking about Miles's kiss again. He'd told her he had feelings for her, and she had feelings for him, but she was too afraid to show them.

She closed her books and decided no more studying for the night. The house was quiet again. The only noise she heard was a faint sound from the television in Rollin and Tayler's room. She slid into her flip-flops and decided to step out for a little air. If she could just get Miles out of her head, maybe she could get something written.

Most nights, Kyla enjoyed sitting out back in the garden gazing into the starlit sky. However, tonight she couldn't see a single star. She could smell rain moving in, but according to the weather man it wouldn't arrive until after midnight. Since she had the time, she decided to stroll down to the gazebo to stretch her legs.

Path lighting led the way to the gazebo, which was bathed by a faint accent light. At night, the gazebo was beautiful. On several occasions they'd hosted beautiful outdoor weddings. A waterproof storage container that was closed and locked held most of her paperwork, keeping it safe from the elements. Small starter pots full of soil were sitting out, waiting to be useful. She grabbed one of the pots and then reached to see what seeds she had around.

"Kind of late to be playing in the dirt, isn't it?"

Kyla jumped and her hand flew to her chest, sending the pot to the floor. She spun around and saw Miles standing in the shadows at the entrance of the gazebo.

"I'm sorry, I thought you heard me coming," he said as he walked over to pick up the pot and set it back on the table.

She took a few deep breaths, then rested her forehead in her palm. "No, I didn't hear anything." She looked up at him. "You scared me to death. I didn't see anybody out here."

"I was still sitting on the porch when I saw somebody walking down the path. I figured it was you. I thought you were studying."

She fumbled with the pot, trying to remember what she was about to plant. "I was working on my dissertation and kind of got stuck. I come out here sometimes when I can't think, to sort of clear my head."

He strolled around the table, nodding. "Yeah, I can see how this would relax you."

She drummed her fingernails against the table. Her stomach quivered, and she could feel Miles watching her. Then she remembered what she'd been doing and found the seed packets on a shelf under the table.

She took in all of his masculinity hovering over her, but she wasn't ready to give up her teacher role just yet. "I know it's late, but do you want to plant some of these non-GMO cilantro seeds with me?"

He laughed and reached for a pot. "I'll have you know that food from GM seeds, like the ones we produce, have the same nutritional characteristics as food from seeds produced through conventional breeding, including organic crops." He reached for the package of seeds she'd left on the table.

"My, my, somebody certainly has brainwashed you. You do know there aren't a lot of people who believe that, don't you?"

"What I do know is that there are a lot of people who live by that fact. It's been proven. You should attend the Global Summit on Food and Beverages we talked about."

She shrugged. "Maybe one day." She finished planting her cilantro and set the pot aside. From under the counter, she pulled out a package of baby wipes and set them in front of her.

Miles finished his pot and pushed it out in front of him. "Does this pass your inspection?"

Kyla picked up the pot and examined it. She turned down her lips. "Not bad, Mr. Parker, not bad at all."

Miles walked around the table until he was standing next to Kyla. She'd opened a package of baby wipes and was pulling one out. He leaned in close to her, and her whole body tensed up in anticipation of another kiss, but he plucked a wipe from the package, instead. She dropped her head and stood there, slightly embarrassed, as she wiped her hands. The sounds of crickets and an old truck going down the road in the distance filled the silence between them.

"I've been wanting to do this all week," Miles said, as he dropped his wipe on the table before he placed both hands behind Kyla's head. Her eyes widened, and she gripped the table with one hand to steady her weakening knees. He held her ponytail with one hand, and slid the holder down with his other hand. Her hair cascaded along her shoulders and down her back. "Damn!"

She gave her head a little shake, releasing her hair from the confines of the ponytail, giving her a free feeling.

Miles ran his hand through her hair, fluffing it out. "Why don't you ever wear it down?"

His touch made her scalp tingle and sent a warm shiver through her body. She swallowed hard. "It's more practical at work to keep it up." Since he wasn't going to kiss her again, she had a mind to reach out and kiss him. He massaged the back of her scalp, pulling her hair down and her chin up until she was looking up into his eyes.

He licked his lips, and she could see the desire in his eyes. He wanted her, and he wanted her bad. Her heartbeat raced, and she fantasized about him pulling her into his chest and wrapping his arms around her. This time when he kissed her, she'd plant one on him that he wasn't likely to forget for the rest of his life.

Instead of kissing her, Miles removed his hand and took a step back. He closed his eyes and ran a hand over his mouth. A nanosecond later, he looked deep into her eyes. "I think I'd better call it a night. Standing out here with you makes me want to forget all about my vow. I want to kiss you again. The only problem is, once I start I know I'm not gonna want to stop."

She took a step back, as well, realizing that her fantasy

wasn't going to come true tonight. She reached for the wipes and tossed them into the garbage can nearby. "You know, I think your vow is a good thing. It takes a strong man to commit to something so...what's the word?"

"Crazy," he said, shaking his head.

She crossed her arms. "It's not really that hard, is it?" She practically lived in a state of celibacy; there'd been no man in her life for a while now.

"It hasn't been...until now," he admitted with a pained expression on his face.

A shiver of pleasure ran through her body. She had to turn her gaze away from him as she tried not to blush. *Could she really do that to a man?* "Well, to help you out, I think I need to get back to studying."

He chuckled. "Yeah, okay. Were you able to clear your head?" he asked.

How could she have cleared her head when he had her so confused right now? They wanted each other, but they couldn't have each other because of his vow, yet he kept getting close to her. She didn't know what to think. "Actually, no, I'm more confused now than when I came out here."

"I'm sorry. That's my fault. I can't hide how I feel about you. When I see you, I want to touch you, hold you and kiss you. Tomorrow is going to be a hard day for me."

She looked down and nodded. "Your shadowing comes to an end."

He reached out for her hand. "Come on. Let's head back up to the house. I think I need a cold shower."

She took his hand, and blushed with happiness as they walked out of the gazebo and back up the path.

Saturday morning, when Kevin drove the truck around to the front of the B and B to pick up the mornings guests, Kyla held her breath. Today was Miles's last day with her and she was already starting to miss him. The guests made their way down the front steps as Kevin stopped the truck. Kyla jumped out to pull the step down from the back of the truck. She introduced herself to a few new guests who'd checked in yesterday as everybody climbed onboard. She didn't see Miles.

Kevin stepped out of the truck and glanced over at her. He'd grown accustomed to talking with Miles every morning, as well. It wasn't too often they had a guest who practically worked the farm all week with them. Kyla shrugged as they glanced from each other to the front porch.

She was just about to walk up to the house when the screen door opened and Miles walked out. She let out a deep breath and turned around, biting down on the inside of her cheek to suppress a smile, but one look at Kevin's smiling face as he opened the driver's door, and she let the smile take over her face. She kept her back to Miles until she regained control of her emotions.

"I almost missed you, didn't I?" Miles said with a big grin on his face as he walked up behind her.

Kyla spun around and looked at her watch. "We were going to give you another few minutes. Can't have you holding up the morning, you know."

He climbed up on the back of the truck. "I wouldn't want to do that." He greeted all the guests as he found a place at the front of the truck.

Kyla grabbed her usual seat, which happened to be next to Miles this morning. She gave Kevin the okay to proceed. After her usual greeting and instructions, she tried to make small talk with a few of the guests in order to keep her eyes off Miles.

He seemed to be doing the same thing, talking to the man next to him. Occasionally she would glance his way to find him staring at her. When he leaned over and touched her leg to get her attention, she almost jumped off her seat.

"Since I'm not staying for dinner, are you going to put my collections in the U-pick store this morning?" he asked.

She nodded. "We can, unless you want to take them with you, which is what guests usually do."

He shook his head. "I'm not going straight home, and besides, there's no way I could cook vegetables anywhere near as good as Mrs. Rita." He leaned in even closer and motioned her forward. "Unless you want to come to my place and cook them for me," he said in her ear.

Kyla's eyes popped, but she tried to hide her surprise by turning her head and adjusting her ponytail. Was he just playing with her? Or had he really just invited her to his home? She shook her head. "Trust me, I don't hold a candle to Aunt Rita. You'd be sorely disappointed."

He straightened up and grinned. "You couldn't disappoint me even if you tried."

Kyla turned her head and blushed. This man had managed to charm even her. How had she fallen under his spell so easily? For the first time ever, she dreaded the first chore of the morning, knowing it would be Miles's last.

The truck came to a stop, and Kyla prepared to make this a memorable morning, if nothing else.

Miles spent more time assisting guests and talking with Kevin than picking vegetables this morning. Once he had the chance, he stood there and marveled at the land, hoping his purchase in Nicholasville would be as beautiful as the land he stood on. Glenda had assured him the property was in good condition, but the farmer couldn't afford to keep it up. He hated to see so many farmers going into debt, then losing their farms anyway. He really wanted to be the solution to someone's problem rather than the problem.

"You're finished for the morning?"

Miles turned around to see the woman who ran through

his dreams each night. "Just taking a break and enjoying the view," he told Kyla.

She looked out across the fields, but he couldn't take his eyes off her.

"Absolutely beautiful," he said, referring to her more than the land.

Kyla turned to him. "It is. Now do you see why I enjoy coming out here every morning? It doesn't matter what mood you're in." She swept her hand in front of her. "This view will lift your spirits. You can even catch a rainbow, after a good rain."

He stared out at the fields of growing produce, sure he'd feel differently about the view if he had to work it every day. For a moment, Kyla stood alongside him with her hands behind her back, looking across the land, as well.

"I wish you could come back with me," he finally said, breaking the silence but keeping his eyes straight ahead.

"No, you don't," Kyla said.

"What do you mean?" he asked, turning to her.

"What you're experiencing is the typical student–teacher crush. The tables were turned this week and I was the authority figure. I know you're not used to that, but it happens. There's been a little harmless flirting going on, but that's it. You made a vow with God and you're sticking to it. You know, I'm very passionate about what I do, and sometimes that passion can be attractive."

He traced her lips as she spoke, not buying a word of it. "But my question is, is the teacher attracted to the student?"

She released her arms and brought a hand up, stroking her throat. She tilted her head towards him. "I think you know the answer to that question."

Every nerve ending in his body stirred as she turned and walked away leaving him weak at the knees.

* * *

With his bag packed and his bill paid, Miles said good-bye to his hosts. "I want to thank you guys for a wonderful experience. I gained an education on growing organic foods that I'll never forget. And tell Mrs. Rita she cooked some of the best food I've ever put in my mouth."

Rollin and Tayler laughed along with Miles.

"Well, now that you know where we are, don't be a stranger," Rollin said.

"Most definitely. I'll be sure to recommend the Coleman House to all my friends. As a matter of fact, I might gift my business partner a week's stay."

Tayler looked up at Rollin, smiling, and then turned back to Miles. "We'll be more than happy to host anyone you send."

Miles cleared his throat. "I didn't really get to say good-bye to Kyla after the truck came back in. Do you know where I can find her?"

"She should be down by the gazebo. Her workshop's about to start," Tayler said.

"Okay, thanks, I'll run down there on my way out. Again, it's been amazing."

After exchanging handshakes, Miles walked out to his SUV and tossed his bag inside, then turned around and headed toward the gazebo.

From a distance, he didn't see anyone there. When he reached the empty gazebo he decided to leave her a note. Before he could find a pen or some paper, he heard laughter coming in his direction. When he turned around, Kyla and several of the B and B guests were coming down the path.

"Miles! I thought you were gone." She entered the gazebo with a big smile on her face and an armful of small herb pots like the ones they'd planted last night.

"I'm on my way out now, but I wanted to say goodbye."

"Are you Miles Parker, the baseball player?" one of the guests asked.

Miles nodded and glanced at the man briefly before turning back to Kyla.

"Cool. Are you taking this workshop, too?" he asked.

Kyla set her pots down. "Mr. Parker was with us all last week. He's learning about organic farming and discovering the many wonderful benefits. Isn't that right, Mr. Parker?"

The fake smile on Kyla's face and the disguised lift to her voice wasn't fooling Miles. Maybe she didn't want these people to know how she felt about him, but something special had happened between them this week that couldn't be denied. "I learned a lot this week. Organic farming is definitely a labor of love. But I also learned a lot about myself and what I really want out of life." Miles stared deep into Kyla's eyes, as if she were the only one in the gazebo.

Her lips parted, and she gave him a hesitant look before asking, "What's that?"

"A woman who shares my passions and dreams of one day ridding the world of hunger. Someone who's not waiting on the government or anybody else to do what needs to be done in this world. That's what I want."

Miles needed to touch her at that moment. He wanted to taste her lips and wrap her in his arms. Once he walked away from here the moment would be lost. He didn't know if he'd ever see her again, but he wanted to make sure she knew how he felt.

He closed the distance between them and wrapped his arm around her waist. "Thank you for the education." He covered her mouth with his, and closed his eyes while savoring the minty taste of her lips.

Suddenly, her body pressed against his while her hand wrapped around his neck. A moment of confusion turned into the realization that Kyla was kissing him back. She'd lost all inhibitions right there in front of her class. His body temperature rose when she opened her mouth and entwined their tongues.

He didn't see, hear or care about anything right now but the woman wrapped in his arms. The sweet taste of her exploded in his mouth and momentary lightheadedness took over. His loins tightened. In front of everyone, she'd let her feelings for him be known in the best way possible. He was so preoccupied with thoughts of kissing her, he hadn't even noticed some of her family members coming down the path.

To a round of applause, she lowered her hands from his chest and slowly pulled away, looking up into his eyes. Unable to find words, he merely stared at her in disbelief.

Chapter 13

The cozy offices of Parker Edmunds Foods occupied space on the fifteenth floor of the PNC Tower in downtown Lexington. Miles ran the entire company from these five rooms. Rarely did anyone come into the office who didn't work there. Unless, on occasions like today, when his attorney, Winston Collier; his brother, Brandon; and a longtime advisor, Ralph McKay, met to discuss business.

"So, everyone's in agreement this is the move we want to make?" Miles asked his business team to confirm before they made a very important acquisition.

Glenda turned her gaze from the window toward the team. "We won't be able to survey the land until the family moves out, but from what we've seen I think it's perfect for soybeans. Anywhere in that area would be good, but with this foreclosure looming, we'd be foolish to pass it up."

"What about the family living there now?" Brandon asked from his corner spot in the room. "What if they refuse to leave? I saw something like that on television."

Miles cleared his throat. "We'll cross that bridge when we come to it. A foreclosure's not an easy thing to come to grips with." He looked at Glenda. "Do you know anything about the family living there?"

She shook her head. "No, but do we need to know anything about them? And I'm not trying to be facetious here, but the acquisition is more my concern."

Winston shuffled some papers in front of him. "I do know that only one person works outside of the farm. That land is the source of most of their income. However, it hasn't produced enough to pay off the loan in years. I believe there are about six residents, two of them children."

Miles shook his head. "I know their well-being is none of my concern, but unless they have someplace to go, this stinks."

Winston, Ralph and Glenda all chimed in at the same time in response to Miles's concerns. He couldn't help how he felt. While doing mission work, he'd watched his father help families who'd lost everything due to drought, conflicts or corruption, with no place to go.

He didn't like the idea of benefiting from someone else's pain.

"Look, at the end of the day, it's business, Miles," Ralph broke through the chatter. "You're not the cause of their pain, and you aren't taking advantage of them. But I understand where you're coming from. If it makes you feel any better, I'll personally look into the owner's situation as best I can."

Miles nodded. Always sympathetic, Ralph, like Miles, had traveled the world as a child and had his own famine stories to tell.

"What's the name of the family?" Ralph asked Winston.

"Montgomery. The name on the deed is Paula Montgomery," Winston confirmed.

Ralph nodded as he jotted it down.

"Okay, the next piece of business to discuss is the Global Summit in Chicago next week," Glenda said. "Everything has been shipped to McCormick Place, reservations have been made for Friday night's dinner and I've booked my hotel, but Miles, I assume you and Brandon will be staying at your condo?"

Miles opened his mouth to respond, but Brandon spoke up before he could get a word out. "I can't go."

Miles turned to his little brother in disbelief. "What do you mean, you can't go? We've been talking about this for months."

Brandon shrugged. "I know, but something's come up."

Miles wanted to know what could be that important, but he didn't want to ask in front of everyone there. "We'll talk after the meeting," was all he said.

They finished discussing all of the business at hand, and thirty minutes later their staff meeting was over. Miles pulled Brandon aside before he could get away.

"So, what's so important?" he asked Brandon.

Brandon shoved his hands into his pants pockets. "I've been invited to Martha's Vineyard for a couple of days by one of my frat brothers."

Miles shook his head.

"Miles, it's an important invitation. He's the president of the Finance Club, and his father is the CEO of Easley Stock Holdings. I could be setting myself up for a great internship. Before I come to work for Parker Edmunds, that is. Not everybody gets an invite. I can always go to the next summit with you. I just couldn't turn this down."

"I understand, but you could have told me before you made the announcement today."

"I'm sorry, I was going to. Can somebody take my place?"

"Don't worry about it. I'll get somebody else to go. You're missing out on a great learning opportunity."

"Yeah, but I'm sure you'll find a way to make up for it," Brandon said with a smile.

"You're damn skippy I will. But first, be sure to finish all the work you're doing with Glenda before you go. And when you return to Atlanta you need to plan to spend some time with Mama before you go back to school."

"Oh, most definitely. I'll spend a good week in the ATL before I head back."

Miles wondered if Brandon had any idea how privileged he was. All of his young life he'd had someone watching out for and taking care of him. Miles was trying to be a father figure, but maybe he wasn't being tough enough on him.

After Brandon, Winston and Ralph left, Miles and Glenda retreated into their respective offices. Now Miles had to find a replacement for Brandon or forfeit his registration fee.

"Miles." Glenda popped her head into his office. "I'm running down to Sawyer's to grab some lunch. Do you want anything?"

"Naw, I'll grab something on my way out. I need to run a few errands."

"Okay, but they've got these huge chocolate chip cookies that you love. Are you sure I can't bring you one?"

He smiled. She knew him so well. "As tempting as that sounds, I'll pass."

"Okay, I'll catch you later."

The minute Glenda walked out, he could smell warm, soft-baked chocolate chip cookies, as if he stood in the dining room of the B and B. He missed the afternoon treats, and he missed Kyla.

Then he sat straight up. Brandon may have handed him an opportunity to see Kyla again.

Kyla was on her knees weeding a row of lettuce when her cell phone rang. She started to ignore it, but remembered Tracee had told her to expect a call from their brother Gavin. She wouldn't tell her why, only that he needed to speak with them when he had a moment.

She peeled off her gloves and pulled the phone from her back pocket. Miles Parker's name was on the screen. She grinned at the phone and immediately stood up. For a minute, she wasn't sure if she should answer or not. She hadn't spoken to Miles since the day she'd embarrassed herself by kissing him in front of everybody.

Before the call went to voice mail she answered it. "Hello."

"Hey, lady, I know it's been over a week, but do you remember me?"

She laughed and turned around to make sure no one was within earshot. "Of course I remember you. To what do I owe the pleasure of this call?"

"Pack your bags."

Kyla creased her brow in confusion. "Do what?"

"As fate would have it, I have an extra ticket to the Global Summit next week. And I'm taking you as my guest."

Kyla couldn't believe her ears. She knew Miles was speaking at the summit, but she never imagined she would have an opportunity to go. She started walking down the row of lettuce. "Uh, wait a minute, is this an invitation for Rooted Beginnings? Because I'm not—"

"No. This is an invitation for Kyla to attend as my guest. Don't worry. I won't put you to work, and you'll have full access to the showroom floor. You can attend as many workshops and sessions as you want. I'll take care of the hotel and the airline ticket. Just say you'll come."

She stood there in the open field with one hand on the phone at her ear and the other on her hip. She didn't know what to say. He was offering her a trip that had been on her wish list ever since she graduated with her master's in agribusiness.

"Kyla," Miles prompted after not getting a response.

She couldn't accept his offer. What did he want in return? Maybe sex? No man offered you such a trip and expected nothing in return. But he was celibate.

"Do you need some time to think it over?" he asked.

She'd never accepted such an invitation from any man. Then again, she'd never known any man with enough money to offer her such a trip. "Ah, yeah, can I have a few days to do that?"

"Sure. I'll go ahead and have your room reserved. If you decide not to go, we can always cancel it. Once you make up your mind I'll email your plane reservations."

She cleared the lump from her throat and held a hand to her chest.

"And Kyla?"

"Uh-huh?"

"Don't disappoint me. I'm looking forward to seeing you again."

Well, she could just drop the phone and faint right now.

"Kyla, are you one hundred percent sure you want to do this?" Tracee asked as she held up a sundress that was lying across Kyla's bed.

"I'm two hundred percent sure." Kyla snatched the dress from her and tossed it onto the pile on top of her suitcase. "You've heard me talking about the Global Summit for years. I even tried to get Rollin to sign up. Attending this conference could be life altering for me."

Tracee crossed her arms. "You know that's not what I'm talking about."

Kyla held out two pairs of sandals, motioning for Tracee to pick.

"The strappy ones. They're sexier."

"Sexy isn't what I was going for." Kyla tossed the flat sandals into the suitcase.

Tracee walked over and picked them up. "Miles Parker invited you to Chicago." She tossed the flats back into Kyla's closet and snatched the strappy ones from her hand. "Sexy is what you want." She placed the strappy sandals on top of the pile.

Kyla shook her head. "I'm not you, Tracee. I don't know how to lure a man. I'm not even sure I want to. I have to just be myself, like it or not."

"Excuse me! After the way you kissed him in front of everybody?" Tracee waved her hands in a wide gesture. "You're not fooling anybody, girl. You want that man. You're just so used to keeping everything so secretive. I'll never understand why you don't like to publicly acknowledge when you're seeing someone."

Kyla shrugged and pulled a few more things out of the closet, tossing them onto the bed. "It's my business. Everybody doesn't need to know."

Tracee sat on the edge of Kyla's bed. "I know what it is. You're afraid of high school all over again. But that was years ago, and that guy was a jerk. Don't be afraid to love again. Trust me, all men aren't like that. You should know that by now."

Kyla stopped sorting through clothes and looked at Tracee. "I'm fully aware of that. But Mama didn't raise no fool, so I'm not putting myself out there like that again."

"Then why are you going to Chicago?"

Kyla's voice lowered. "To attend the Summit, and... I guess to see Miles again." She sat down on the other side of the bed.

Tracee took a deep breath. "Kyla, just be careful. I know you two got to know each other pretty well in a week's time, but Miles isn't one of these country boys hanging around here. He might live in Lexington, but he's been living in another world for a long time. A world of beautiful rich people that you know nothing about."

Kyla lifted her chin, about to protest.

Tracee held a hand up. "I don't want you to get hurt. That's all I'm saying. You're my little sister."

Kyla's throat thickened as she swallowed a lump. Tracee was the more emotional one, not her, so why was she about to cry? She took a deep breath and blinked back the tears. "Trust me, I won't do anything you wouldn't do."

"Oh, my God!" Tracee laughed and fell back onto Kyla's pillow. "Don't you even come close to doing anything I would do."

Kyla leaned back onto the other pillow, happy to have this moment with her sister, something that they hadn't had in a long time. "No, seriously, Tracee, I can take care of myself. He's putting me up in a hotel. It's not like I'm staying with him. Besides, I trust him."

Tracee's hand moved across the bed, taking Kyla's. "Yeah, I know you do. So if anything doesn't feel right at any moment, call me. I'll be on the next flight to Chicago."

Kyla squeezed Tracee's hand in return. "Corra told me the same thing earlier."

"That's because we're here for you, all of us. Wait until I tell Mama where you're going."

Kyla let go of Tracee's hand and sat up. "Don't do that."

"Why not?" Tracee asked, sitting up.

"I don't want to worry her. The last time Gavin was here I had the feeling something wasn't right at home. But I've been too busy to go visit. Mama's gonna kill me."

"She'll be okay. I'm meeting with Gavin tomorrow. He wants to talk to me about something. So you go to Chicago and have yourself a ball. Everything and everybody will be right here waiting for you when you come back."

Kyla grabbed Tracee's hand and squeezed. She'd always felt such overwhelming love from her family. "I know you will. That's why I love you guys so much."

Chapter 14

A week later, Kyla made her way to the baggage area at O'Hare airport and looked around for Brandon, who Miles had said would pick her up. She felt a tap on the shoulder, turned around and looked into Brandon's smiling face.

"Hi, Kyla." Brandon gave Kyla a quick hug.

"Brandon, I'm so glad to see you."

He laughed. "Yeah, you were looking a little lost there."

"This is a huge airport."

He shrugged. "Yeah, it's pretty big. Come on, let me help you get your bags."

Kyla followed Brandon to get her luggage and then out to the parking lot. He stopped at a black Porsche Cayenne and raised the trunk. "Have you been to Chicago before?" he asked as he placed her suitcase in the back, then opened the passenger door for her.

"No, I haven't."

"Oh, you're gonna love it. Summer's the best time to be

here." After helping her in, he closed the door and walked around to the driver's side.

"Is this Miles's car?" she asked, once he was inside.

"Yeah, he lets me drive it if I'm running an errand for him or something like that. So, if you don't mind, we'll take the scenic route back."

Kyla laughed. "I don't mind at all."

They chatted all the way to what she thought was going to be her hotel. However, Brandon turned into a high-rise and pushed a button in the car to open the garage.

"Is this the hotel?" she asked.

"No, we're at Lincoln Park, Miles's place. I'm supposed to drop you off and he'll take you to the hotel. Some emergency came up that he had to take care of." Brandon wound the SUV masterfully around the winding garage and pulled into a space marked PARKER.

Once inside, she discovered that the condo came with a gym, a swimming pool and a doorman who knew Brandon by his first name, which Brandon told Kyla was pretty cool. They took the elevator up to the fifteenth floor. Kyla was so impressed with the five-star-hotel feel of the building, she almost forgot they were walking into someone's home.

Brandon opened the door, and the minute she walked in behind him, the stunning floor-to-ceiling view took her breath away. The wall across from the living room was all glass. No curtains, just glass and a beautiful lake view. She immediately walked over and looked down.

"Awesome isn't it?" Brandon asked as he walked up behind her.

She took a deep breath. "This is beautiful."

"Wait until you see it at night," he said with enthusiasm.

Kyla glanced at him. She had no intention of being in this apartment at night.

He shrugged one shoulder. "I mean, if you get a chance."

Kyla spun around when she heard Miles walking into

the room. He looked rather handsome in a pair of stylish distressed jeans and a blue-and-white button-down shirt with the sleeves rolled up, showing off his silver wrist-watch. He was still on the phone talking when he looked at her with wide eyes. She met him halfway, reaching out her hand, but remained silent to respect his phone call. He kept talking while accepting her hand and pulling her in for a hug. Then he gave her a quick kiss on the forehead.

He held the phone against his chest. "I'm sorry, this is just about over with. Have a look around. I hope you don't mind that I had Brandon pick you up?"

She shook her head. "No, not at all. He showed me the city."

"That's good," Miles said before walking over to Brandon and holding his hand out. Brandon fished the keys from his pocket and dropped them into Miles's waiting hand.

"Would you like something to drink?" Miles asked. Before she could answer, he turned to Brandon. "Fix her something." Then he reached out and touched the hair cascading around her shoulders. "I like it," he whispered.

She smiled, knowing that he would.

He returned to his phone call and disappeared down the hall again.

Brandon gave Kyla a bottle of water before giving her a tour of the three-bedroom condo, skipping Miles's office. Two of the bedrooms had the same floor-to-ceiling views of the lake and were filled with artifacts from Miles's travels. When they returned to the living room, Miles was off the phone and sitting on the sofa.

He smiled as he asked her to have a seat. She had an empty feeling in the pit of her stomach, partly due to nerves and partly due to hunger. She also had on a pair of jeans, wedge heels and her favorite gray one-shoulder, slouchy T-shirt. She walked over and took a seat on the other end of the sofa.

"You look good," he said with a smile.

"Thank you. So do you. No cargo shorts," she observed.

He laughed. "No, I thought I'd let you know I do have more than those damn shorts."

"I love your condo. And that view is amazing." From her angle on the sofa now, she could see the tops of buildings and a blue sky.

He turned and looked out at the view. "That's what sold me. I can see Far North, the Navy Pier and even around to the south side on a clear day."

She took a sip of her water and a deep breath to calm her nerves. Okay, why was he so relaxed? As much as she liked the condo, and him, she had no plans to stay here—she was going to her hotel. "So, when does the summit start?" she asked, wanting to convey that she knew exactly why she was there.

"Tomorrow morning. I had to get a new badge for you. We'll pick it up at the registration desk." He stood up. "I have a list of all the workshops if you want to check it out."

"Yeah, I have it here." She pulled the list she'd printed from the internet out of her purse.

Miles stopped, looking as if he didn't think she'd be this prepared. "Oh, okay. I guess you're ready, then."

She noticed that Brandon had left the room. "Yes, I am. And, again, I don't know how to thank you for the invitation. You're probably the only one who knows how much this means to me." She scooted to the edge of the sofa, letting him know she was indeed ready to go.

"I'm happy you accepted my invitation. It feels like I haven't seen you in months, yet it's only been, what?"

"Two weeks," she replied, maybe a little too quickly.

He grinned. "Yes, a long two weeks. But you're here now. Are you hungry?"

"I could eat something," she replied and glanced into his shiny, modern kitchen. "With a kitchen that shiny, do you cook?"

Miles laughed. "Breakfast is about the only thing I can make. Believe me, you don't want me to cook you anything else. I don't want this to be your last visit."

She smiled along with him. If she was being honest with herself, she didn't want this to be her last visit, either.

Miles had booked Kyla a room at the Wyndham on the riverfront for three nights. The hotel was close to the Magnificent Mile, should she want to go shopping. He knew she'd also enjoy the river view from her room. The hotel was enough to impress any first-time Chicago visitor, and he did want to impress her. Once she'd accepted his invitation, he made dinner and tour plans. He was proud of the city that had been so good to him. In the next couple of days, he planned to give her an experience she'd never forget.

Saturday morning, the vendors had to be at the center early, so Miles stopped for coffee for him and tea for Kyla. When he picked her up at the hotel, she walked out in a gray pantsuit with her purse on her arm and her hair blowing in the wind. She looked absolutely stunning.

"Somebody looks as if she had a good night's sleep," he said as she climbed into his SUV.

She blushed. "I have to admit that bed was heavenly. I slept like a baby."

He picked up her tea. "For you," he said, offering her the cup.

Kyla blinked back her surprise. "You stopped and got me something?"

"Herbal tea. I didn't know if you like it sweet or not, so there's a couple packs of sweetener in the console. I remember you don't drink coffee."

He pulled out of the hotel's lot and headed for Mc-Cormick Place. "The conference center isn't far away. My business team will meet us there. I'm only speaking today and attending a few meetings, but the booth will be manned throughout the conference. Don't feel like you have to stay at my booth. Like I promised, your pass gives you full access to all the workshops and every session. Do what you'd normally do if you came to represent Rooted Beginnings. Only your badge will have Parker Edmunds on it."

"I don't care what it has on it as long as I have access to everything. I can explain the situation. I'm also looking forward to meeting your business partner."

He smiled and glanced out the window. "I'm sure the feeling's mutual." The minute he'd told Glenda he had invited Kyla, she seemed eager to meet her.

After making their way through registration, the opening ceremony and introductions, Miles politely posed for several photographs before he caught up with Glenda and their team.

"Do all of these people work for you?" Kyla asked as they approached his booth.

"No, we're a small company. Glenda hires a few of these kids all the time to work shows like this. Let me introduce you."

Unlike Kyla in her flats, Glenda wore heels, dress slacks and a feminine blazer with the sleeves pushed up. She looked professional, yet she still managed to give off a supermodel vibe. She was busy giving out instructions to the temporary help as they walked up.

She did a double take and stopped talking the minute she noticed Kyla beside Miles.

"Miles, there you are. I wondered what happened to you after the opening ceremony. One minute I saw you across the room, and the next you were gone. And this must be Kayla, is it?" Glenda asked, not once looking at Miles while offering her hand to Kyla.

"It's Kyla, no A." Kyla accepted her hand.

"Kyla," Glenda repeated. "Well, it's nice to meet you. I'm the other half of Parker Edmunds. You might say I'm the brains of this outfit. I just use Miles for his good looks."

Miles crossed his arms and pretended to pout.

Kyla tilted her head up at him. "How's that working out? Business kind of slow?"

The three of them shared a good laugh.

"Glenda, it's a pleasure meeting you, as well. And thank you for not objecting to me attending in Brandon's place. I've wanted to attend this Summit for a very long time."

"That's what Miles told me. You are more than welcome."

"You know, Miles never told me his partner was a woman," Kyla added.

Glenda reached out and swatted Miles on the arm. "Shame on you."

Miles shrugged. "It never came up. I was busy digging in the dirt."

"Imagine my surprise when Miles told me he was spending a week on a farm. I wish I could have seen him planting vegetables. You tried to turn him into a real farmer, didn't you?"

Kyla laughed. "He wanted to learn about organic produce, so I tried to teach him something. I'm not sure he's ready to be a farmer just yet, though."

Glenda rested her hands on her hips. "But you did something I doubt any woman's been able to do in a long time. You held his attention. He came back here talking my head off about what he learned. And that's saying a lot, because he's not that much of a talker."

Miles didn't know if he agreed with that. He was a talker.

"Is Danville your home?" Glenda asked, lowering her hands.

"No, I'm from Nicholasville, originally. That's my cousin's farm in Danville."

"Really? We're looking into purchasing some property in Nicholasville. God has blessed us with the ability to expand, and land is cheaper there than Lexington. We're hoping to turn the property into something that sustains more people in the long run," Glenda said.

Kyla's erect posture and the serious look that came over her face told Miles this conversation was about to go south if he didn't step in. Kyla wasn't a fan of their products. One thing he did like was that they were getting along great. "Okay ladies, enough of the idle chit-chat. It's time to educate the crowd and do a little networking. And in honor of this being Kyla's first trip to Chicago, lunch at Luno's is on me."

"That place is going to be packed on a day like this. Do you think we'll be able to get in?" Glenda asked.

"Already taken care of. Just plan to meet right here at noon," Miles instructed.

Glenda winked at Kyla. "That's another reason I keep him around. His celebrity status gets us some of the best tables in town." Glenda glanced at her watch. "I'm going to work the floor a bit. Miles, I'll meet you back here in time for our first meeting." Glenda waved and headed off.

"So, have you mapped out what you want to attend?" Miles asked Kyla. He'd seen her studying the program during the opening ceremony.

"Yes, somewhat, anyway. First, I need to find Urban Agriculture for Sustainable Livelihood, then there's a host of others after that. So I'll be back at noon."

She looked happier than Miles had ever seen her. To know that he'd done something to put that glow on her face made him feel good. "See you at noon."

* * *

Chicago-style, vegetarian deep-dish pizza was now Kyla's favorite food, organic or not. While they ate, Glenda entertained her with stories about Parker Edmunds stumbling to get off the ground. Like Kyla and Miles, Glenda had her own stories of witnessing hunger and needing to do something about it. Over lunch, Kyla came to the conclusion that she really liked Glenda. So when the conference was over and Glenda confirmed dinner plans with Miles, Kyla was excited about going.

As the sun set, they pulled up to Riva Crab House on the Navy Pier. A little tired from her day, Kyla sat straight up when she saw all the excitement going on at the pier. It reminded her of an amusement park without the rides. Miles valet parked his SUV and held her hand as they walked inside the restaurant.

Once inside, Glenda introduced her to Quan, a very tall, handsome, older man, who Miles whispered was Glenda's new gentleman friend, a philanthropist she'd met on a trip to South America.

The level of intellectual conversation that transpired around the table was both stimulating and refreshing to Kyla. She was seeing yet another side of Miles, one that was even more impressive than what he'd already shared with her. Their steak and seafood dinner lasted well into the night as their floor-to-ceiling view of the lake changed from dusk to complete darkness. Miles had ordered a bottle of champagne, of which Kyla had had one glass. She wasn't a big drinker, and now wasn't the time to start.

After dinner, the decision was made to take the little party to Miles's Lincoln Park condo for a nightcap. Kyla wasn't sure that was a good idea. She shivered a little, remembering the way she'd kissed him on his last day at the B and B.

He gazed at her with raised brows as if asking for her

approval. Since she wouldn't be there with him alone, she decided to go with the flow. She gave him a slight nod of her head, hoping she wasn't walking into dangerous territory.

Chapter 15

"You don't mind coming in for a little while do you?" Miles asked as he pulled into his garage.

Although it was about her bedtime, this was a once-in-a-lifetime experience for Kyla, and she could sleep when she got home. "No, I'm fine. I've had such a good time today, I hate to see it come to an end."

Miles reached over and squeezed Kyla's hand. "Yeah, me, too."

The doorman greeted Miles, then tipped his hat and smiled at Kyla. "It's a pleasure to see you again Ms. Kyla."

She smiled back and now understood why Brandon liked the personalized greeting so much. It made her feel welcome. "Thank you, and you, as well."

Once they were on the elevator, Miles let go of her hand and wrapped his around her waist, stepping closer until their foreheads touched. "How does he know your name?" he asked.

The butterflies in her stomach took off. She bit her bottom lip so he couldn't see it trembling. "Brandon introduced us yesterday."

She was becoming comfortable around Miles, which was a dangerous thing. They obviously had feelings for each other, but if he knew how much she'd fallen for the Miles Parker charm, he'd wish he'd never made that vow.

Miles pulled his head back and looked down at her. "I think he likes you. He normally just grins."

"You mean, he grins at all the women you bring up here," she said, as the elevator stopped and opened on the fifteenth floor.

Miles licked his lips and what she perceived as a cocky smile spread across his face. They stepped off the elevator. "I haven't entertained a woman in my condo in over a year, maybe longer." As they walked down the corridor, he glanced over at her. "So, no. What I meant was, he grins at anybody who comes up with me. Other than Brandon, of course, because he stands down there asking him all kinds of questions."

They reached Miles's apartment and he opened the door. The cool air hit Kyla the minute she walked in. Her eyes were immediately drawn to the giant windows and the blackness, with speckles of light coming from the city below. She couldn't help herself; she walked over and touched the glass.

She closed her eyes, listening to the soft R & B music that was piped throughout the condo. This was heaven. This day, this evening with Miles, was something she never would have dreamed possible the first time she'd met him. She flinched and opened her eyes when he placed his arm around her shoulders and stared out the window.

"Beautiful night, isn't it?" he said. His voice was huskier than before. She lowered her hands. "It's so beautiful, I wanted to reach out and touch it." She glanced up at him. "I'm sorry, I got fingerprints on your glass."

He shook his head. "Don't worry about that. My house-keeper comes in once a week and wipes them down. Touch it again if you want to. Put your whole hand up there." He removed his arm from her shoulders and stood behind her, taking both hands into his and placing her palms flat against the cool glass.

Kyla shook her head. "She's going to wonder what the hell you were doing in here."

He leaned closer until his body touched hers. Then his breath against her neck sent a tingle throughout her whole body. He whispered in her ear, "I know what I want to be doing in here." He kissed her neck while holding his palms flat against the backs of her hands.

Long suppressed sexual urges rose up in Kyla in a way she'd never expected. Her head fell back into the crook of Miles's neck as he continued to whisper in her ear.

"You taught me some things about vegetables, but I'd like to teach you some—"

The doorbell rang.

"Ugh," Miles grunted and lowered his face into Kyla's neck.

She hadn't realized she'd been holding her breath until just then. She released a deep sigh.

Miles removed his hands and took a step back. "Glenda and Quan, I damn near forgot about them."

Kyla lowered her hands and turned around. She'd forgotten about them, as well.

Miles reached out and caressed the side of her jaw. "I could always tell them to go away. Or better yet, pretend we're not here and don't answer the door."

The smoldering look in his eyes said they were about to get into trouble if he didn't answer the door. "I think you should answer it. I mean, you just invited them over." What they needed right now was a diversion.

The doorbell rang again. He lowered his head, placing his mouth on Kyla's. She held onto Miles's shirt, too afraid to completely pull him in. After a quick but nice kiss, he stepped back.

She noticed Miles adjusting himself as he crossed the room. Arousing him had not been her intention, so she hoped he was thankful for the interruption. She sat on the sofa and leaned back, trying to look relaxed.

"Well, it's about time," Glenda said as she strutted in. "We were beginning to think you'd changed your mind." Quan strode in behind Glenda, smiling like he'd won the lottery.

"No, not at all, come on in. I was uh...just giving Kyla a little tour," Miles lied as his guests entered.

While Miles went into the kitchen to prepare drinks, Kyla had the opportunity to chat with Quan. She learned more about his philanthropic work as well as his interest in agriculture and farming.

The foursome resumed their dinner conversation until the doorbell rang again. This time, Glenda opened the door and another couple walked in. Miles introduced Winston, his lawyer, and his wife. They'd just happened to be in the area, so Glenda had invited them over. For the next two hours they drank, talked politics, and tried to solve the world's problems.

Kyla could feel her eyelids getting heavier, but hadn't realized she'd dozed off until her body leaned into Miles's. He sat next to her in the middle of a serious debate about why the U.S. didn't help Africa more. She quickly righted herself, pretending she'd wanted to snuggle up next to him.

"Are you okay?" Miles asked, as he sat back and placed his arm around her shoulders.

She slid into the spot between his chest and arm as if she was meant to be there. She nodded and tried to look awake, but her eyelids were so heavy.

"No, you're not. What would you be doing if you were home right now?" he asked.

The other couples continued to chat as if they hadn't noticed Miles pull away from the conversation. Kyla lifted his wrist and looked at his watch. "At a quarter to twelve I'd probably be under the covers." She held a hand over her mouth to stifle a yawn.

He leaned in and whispered in her ear, "That sounds like an invitation."

Kyla bit her bottom lip. As much as she would love to stay with Miles tonight, she didn't want to be the cause of his breaking his vow. "I didn't mean for it to be."

"I know you didn't. That's what I like about you."

Glenda moved from her chair to the arm of Quan's and then leaned over to whisper in his ear. They looked in Kyla's direction, but she was too tired to care what they were saying.

"Well, folks, Quan and I are going to call it a night. I have to be back at McCormick Place by nine, so I need to get some sleep." Glenda stood up.

"We're right behind you," Winston said as he stood and reached down to help his wife up.

Everyone was leaving. Kyla sat up, instantly wide awake. *They're about to leave me alone with Miles!*

Glenda gave Kyla a hug. "I'll see you in the morning." Then she released her and held her at arm's length. "Get a good night's sleep."

"I think I've already started," Kyla said, referring to her nodding off.

Glenda held a hand up, shielding her response from the rest of the group. "I noticed."

Kyla shrugged. So much for her efforts to look engaged. After hugs all around, Miles walked everyone to the door. While he was there, Kyla scooped up the glasses from the table and carried them into the kitchen. There was no way she could repay him for the conference, but she could show her appreciation by cleaning up.

Under the sink she found the dish liquid and started washing the glasses. She knew when Miles returned he'd tell her to stop, so she hurried.

"You don't have to do that," Miles said as he walked up behind her. "I told you, I have a housekeeper. All I have to do is place them in the dishwasher."

She shrugged. "I know, but it makes me feel better to do something after—" Kyla flinched as Miles's hands slid down her arms and his body pressed against her back. "What are you doing?"

His hands found hers under the water. "Helping you wash glasses," he responded in his husky voice.

The heat from his body prevented her from thinking straight. She released the glasses as their fingers intertwined. Miles slowly caressed her hands while kissing his way down her neck. She closed her eyes and tilted her head to the side, giving him full access, hoping he wouldn't stop there.

"Did you enjoy yourself today?" he asked, his lips inches from her ear.

She tried to speak, but found it hard to form a sentence. *What is this man doing to me?* With every breath, her whole upper body rose and fell. She nodded and uttered, "Uh-huh."

He whispered in her ear, "Watching you do the dishes is kind of sexy."

Kyla let her head rest on his chest again and took a deep breath. *And doing dishes like this is almost unbearable.* "I've never heard anyone…refer to washing dishes…as sexy," she said between breaths.

"Then maybe just having you here is what's turning me on," he replied before kissing the top of her head. His hands gradually rose from the water and rested on the edge of the sink. When she turned her head to look at him, he leaned in slowly, and her body trembled in anticipation. His warm breath met her lips as his tongue sought her mouth. She forgot all about the damn glasses.

He kissed her in such an urgent fashion that they both forgot their hands were wet. He moved to the side of her and pulled her hands out of the water, wrapping them around his neck.

Her desire for Miles was something she'd been struggling with from the minute she'd laid eyes on him. Miles was unlike any other man she'd ever met, and the more time she spent with him, the more she wanted him. A little voice in the back of her head told her to slow down and remember his vow, but the fire growing inside of her was so powerful she ignored the voice and caressed his head in her hands.

Miles devoured her mouth, kissing her as if this was the last time they'd ever see each other. He turned her completely around with her back to the counter. Her legs were slightly parted, and he wedged one leg right in against her heat. His growing erection pressed against her pelvic bone. He moaned several times as he pressed his thigh into her, forcing her legs wider apart. Suddenly, he released her mouth and took a step back.

She readjusted her stance while catching her breath. Miles breathed as if he'd just run a marathon. He collapsed against her again and dropped his head into her neck.

"Kyla." He whispered her name in a strained voice that she didn't recognize.

She knew he struggled with his desire to make love to her and his desire to keep his vow, but the breathless way in which he said her name drove her crazy. She pulled up his shirt until it was out of his pants. He stepped back again and she started working on the buttons. She needed to touch his naked chest and then wrap her arms around his body. Miles put a hand under her chin, raising her face until he captured her mouth again.

She undid the last button and threw his shirt open. *Sweet Jesus!* There was his magnificent chest again, scar and all. He lowered his arms as she pulled the shirt down until it landed on the kitchen floor.

He ignored the shirt and wrapped his hands around her waist, pulling her away from the counter, closer to him. Kyla's hands slid around his waist. They stood there, holding each other, breathing deep, afraid of what came next. She waited for him to make the next move, but she knew what she wanted him to do.

Instead, Miles took a deep cleansing breath and lowered his head. "I think I'd better take you to your hotel."

She squeezed her eyes tight. *No!* Her body craved his touch, caresses, kisses and anything else he wanted to do to her. She'd fantasized about their lovemaking almost every night.

Miles stepped back and stared down at her, tracing her face with his eyes. She lowered her arms and looked away, unable to take the tempting rise and fall of his chest. He picked his shirt up from the floor.

"I don't know what I was thinking, bringing you up here in the first place." He reached out and pinched her chin between his fingers. "I know how weak I get when I'm around you," he admitted in a low tone.

Kyla took his offered hand, and he led her back to the sofa. She understood his struggle, but she was having one of her very own. "You just wanted to extend the dinner party. You probably weren't even thinking about me at the time."

He stopped and turned to her. "I'm always thinking about you."

The flutter in her stomach subsided as she reached for her purse. Miles put his shirt back on but left it hanging outside of his pants. "Let me grab my keys," he said, then turned around and ran into the side table, swearing at himself as he held his knee.

He snatched up his keys from a bowl sitting near the edge of the kitchen counter and walked toward the door. Kyla followed him, hoping he wasn't mad at her for tempting him. Since he'd turned her on, as well, and had her panties soaking wet, she figured they were even.

He stood holding the doorknob. "I uh... I—"

"Miles, you don't have to say anything. I respect the vow you've made, and I totally understand."

He tilted his head, and the corners of his lips turned up slightly. "I made that vow in good faith, waiting for the right woman to come along."

"I know. I didn't mean to tempt you," she explained.

He lowered his head and opened the door. Kyla took a step, and then Miles took her by the arm and pulled her back. He closed the door.

"I don't want you to go," he said, as he took her hand into his. And then he looked up into her eyes. "I mean, unless you want to go. But if you want to stay...do you want to stay?"

The vulnerable look in Miles's eyes rendered Kyla incapable of resisting his offer. "I do, but—"

Miles didn't wait to hear what else she had to say. He wrapped her arm around his waist and cupped her face in the palms of his hands. When he leaned down for a kiss, her mind exploded with excitement and desire. Her purse fell to the floor as she returned the passion-filled kiss. Moans escaped from deep within his throat, weakening her knees. Her pulse raced as a euphoric feeling spread throughout her body.

Miles picked her up, and she wrapped her legs around his body. The slow R & B soundtrack in the background added fuel to the fire. He carried her into his bedroom and laid her on her back before coming down on top of her. Realizing her fantasy was about to come true, she reached up to unbutton his shirt, then unbuckled his pants and stripped off his belt. The whole time, they never stopped tasting each other. Once she unzipped his pants, he tore at them, pushing them down and off.

He leaned over and slowly helped her out of her pants while caressing and kissing her all over. He moved back up and slid her bra straps off her shoulders as his lips branded their way down her breast to her nipple. He teased her body until she couldn't take it any longer. He eased his body down next to her, facing her, and gazed into her eyes for a couple of seconds. She reached for his hand and interlocked their fingers, holding them up as he stared at their hands. She could see in his eyes that he was ready to make love to her, and she hoped he could see that she was ready to give herself to him.

Miles brought her hand to his mouth and kissed her knuckles before he sat up, lowering his feet to the floor. She wanted to ask him if he was sure about this, but all she could do was run her hand down his back. It was selfish, she knew, but she had to have him. He leaned over and opened the nightstand drawer.

When he turned back around, he had a condom in his hand. She was on her knees now, caressing his chest and yearning for him to kiss her again. In one swift move, he held her by her behind and brought her legs around him until she straddled him. She wrapped her arms around his neck and ground her pelvis against his enormous erection. She rocked against him while he squeezed her behind, pulling her closer against him. She threw her head back, searching for air; she was so hot she couldn't breathe.

Miles kissed her neck, collarbone and chest as she arched her back, giving him better access to her breast. He left her breathless and lightheaded as he released her breast, picked her up, turned around and positioned her on her back. With her legs spread, he massaged between her legs with the palm of his hand before spreading her lips and teasing her soaking-wet clit. She closed her eyes and stretched her arms out across his bed, which smelled of clean linen and lavender. Her body jumped as her muscles contracted. Miles removed his hand and ran it up her stomach to caress her breast. Then he opened the condom package and slowly rolled it down his shaft. Kyla couldn't take her eyes off him, she wanted him so bad.

When he slid between her legs, she could feel his body trembling. He hesitated before entering her, so she reached out with both hands and caressed the sides of his face before running her hands behind his neck. He lowered his head and she sucked his bottom lip into her mouth and kissed him as he slowly entered her, stretching her to accommodate him. Kyla opened her mouth, taking deep breaths, allowing her body to adjust to something she hadn't had in so long.

Miles's jaw was set and his eyes were smoldering as he looked down into her eyes. "Wrap your legs around me," he said in a hoarse voice that she hoped to hear often.

She did as instructed, and he stroked slow and steady until she'd taken all of him. Then he stole her heart as he whispered in her ear, saying how much he wanted her as they made love. She ran her hands up and down his back before holding on, as his thrusts became deeper and faster. He took her on a ride to heaven and back, while changing positions a few times along the way.

When she came down to earth, Miles lay behind her, holding her snugly in his arms. They lay there spooning as their breathing returned to normal and the music relaxed their bodies. He got up, made a quick bathroom run and came back to her.

Kyla could almost feel her body glowing. She tingled

all over from the pleasurable sensations Miles had brought her over and over again. He kissed the top of her head and pulled her even closer to him, if that was possible.

"You are an amazing woman, do you know that?" he asked.

She squeezed her eyes closed. What they had just done had caused him to break his vow. A vow he'd made to God. "I don't feel amazing. I feel horrible. Miles, I'm so sorry." The bed moved as he sat up.

With furrowed brows he asked, "What are you sorry about?"

"We broke your vow. If I hadn't come here, this would never have happened."

He smiled and shook his head. "Baby, I broke my vow because I've found the right woman. You!"

Chapter 16

Miles successfully talked Kyla into moving her departure from Sunday evening to Wednesday morning, while at the same time moving from the Wyndham to his Lincoln Park address.

When she arrived at the summit on Sunday, she sucked up every workshop, lecture and networking opportunity that she could. At the end of the afternoon, she was helping Miles's interns take down the Parker Edmunds booth when Miles walked up behind her. "Was it everything you thought it would be?" he asked, with his mouth practically in her ear.

Startled, she jumped and turned around. A devilish smile took over her face. "Are you talking about last night or this morning?" she asked, referring to the love they'd made again this morning before jumping in the shower.

"Ah." He wiggled his index finger at her and shook his head. "I was referring to the summit. I think I know how you feel about everything else."

She cocked her head to the side, then folded her arms. "And how do you know this?" she asked.

He picked up a box of brochures that were on the table next to her and, as if in passing, leaned into her ear. "The same way my neighbors know—by your screams of passion."

She popped him in the arm.

He unsuccessfully tried to dodge her. "Hey, now's not the time to play rough," he said with a big grin plastered on his face. "Wait until we get home."

With her arms folded and her eyes squinted, Kyla watched him join the interns, thanking them for everything and handing over the box of brochures. She wanted to pinch herself to see if all of this was real. She was standing in a booth that represented genetically modified produce and had spent the night making love to the owner. When he checked into the B and B, her goal had been to win him over to organic produce, and instead, he'd won her heart. All of his charm, talents and good looks were real. She didn't see him as the playboy the papers made him out to be.

With the booth almost wrapped up, Miles rejoined Kyla. "They're going to wait on Glenda, who's doing some last-minute networking. But if you're ready, we can leave." He looked down at his watch. "I need to stop by the Cubs baseball camp this afternoon. Would you like to go with me?"

Kyla's eyes popped. "Yes! Is it okay if you bring somebody? I would love to watch you out there with those kids." He'd told her all about the camp and how he volunteered to stop by for a couple of hours. He'd even thought of opening his own baseball camp for kids.

He laughed. "Yeah, it's cool. Plus, there's somebody I want you to meet."

On their way out of the building they bumped into several fans who stopped Miles for his autograph. It wasn't until times like this that Kyla remembered he was a celebrity.

"I see you're still pretty popular around here, too," Kyla said.

Miles shrugged. "Some people still remember me."

After they left McCormick Place, Miles drove over to the Wyndham where he checked Kyla out and placed her luggage in his trunk. The next stop was Wrigley Field. She spent the next two hours watching and listening to retired third baseman Miles Parker turn into a teacher. The kids loved him, just like Jamie had. Miles was a natural teacher.

Before they left the field, he walked her into the clubhouse and gave her a private tour.

Kyla had never seen anything like it. Everything a player needed was in there. He explained it all to her before an older black gentleman appeared from a back room.

"Captain!" Miles released her hand and walked over to give the older man a big hug.

"Well, if it ain't Parker!" He hugged Miles back, then stood back to look at him. "You lookin' good boy. I saw you out there tossing balls to them kids. You still got it."

Miles laughed and took a step back. "I don't know about that, but how are you getting along?"

"I'm still here, ain't I? They ain't saw fit to kick the old man out yet. I'm still the," he made air quotes with his fingers, "honorary assistant clubhouse manager, so I'm making sure everything's in shape, and taking care of the guys."

Miles reached for Kyla's hand and pulled her forward. "Captain, I want you to meet somebody. This is Kyla Coleman."

Captain smiled, and Kyla noticed a missing tooth. If she had to guess, she'd say he was around seventy-five years old, and he had a wise face. She offered her hand in greeting.

"It's always a pleasure to meet one of Miles's friends. And I see he's given you the grand tour."

"He has." Kyla smiled at Miles wondering what Captain had meant by "one of Miles friends." How many friends or girlfriends had he given this tour to? "This place is amazing. I've never been in a baseball clubhouse before."

"Well, other than reporters, not many wives or girl-friends have graced these doors." Captain smiled up at Miles.

"Hey, Cap, you got any promotional gear back there you can give Kyla for her nephew? He's a future Cubs player, for sure."

Kyla turned from Miles to Captain with raised brows. She hadn't even thought of taking something back for Jamie.

Captain nodded. "Let me see what I can do for you."

He disappeared into a back room, and Kyla turned to Miles, yanking his arm. "Miles, thank you. You think of everything. Jamie is going to be so thrilled. I hope he gives me something I can give to Katie, as well."

Miles gave her a soft kiss on the forehead. "Don't worry, Captain always takes care of me. When I was hurt, he made sure I had everything I needed. And anytime I vol-unteered with a kids' organization, Captain always made sure I got the best promotional stuff. He's always looked out for me that way."

Kyla tilted her head and studied Miles for a second. "He sounds like a good man."

"He is," Miles replied.

Captain returned with a medium-sized duffel bag. "Here you go. This should help to make the little fella a Cubs fan for life."

Miles took the bag. "Captain, I can always count on you being here to take care of me."

Captain slapped Miles's shoulder. "They don't make them like you anymore, Parker. When you got here, you spent more time on the field and in this clubhouse than any other player. These players today are in and out of here so fast it's hard to get to know them." Captain turned and addressed Kyla. "This one used to ask me all kind of questions. We'd spend hours talking religion, politics, the state of the world, and anything else that was on his mind at the time." He frowned. "These new boys are too busy checking their phones all the damned time."

"Captain, I'm gonna come back one day soon, and we'll have an old-fashioned sit-down."

"You do that. You know where to find me. Young lady, it was nice meeting you. I know you must be pretty special for Miles to bring you down here. This is sacred territory to him."

"Really! Then I'm privileged to have met you Captain, and thanks for everything," she said, pointing to the bag on Miles's shoulder. The bag she couldn't wait to open.

Miles and Captain said their goodbyes, and they left the clubhouse.

On their way to the car, Kyla didn't mention Captain's reference to Miles's friends, but couldn't help but wonder what number friend she was.

"Miles, thank you for letting me tag along today. I've never been a baseball fan, but today has been such an eye opener I may sit down and watch a game with Jamie when I get home."

Miles laughed. "This is just the beginning. I'm going to introduce you to baseball the same way you introduced me to organic veggies." He winked at her. "You know, a hands on approach."

She bit down on the inside of her jaw. "I didn't say I wanted to play baseball, only watch it."

He wiggled his index finger at her. "Oh, no, you have to get your hands dirty to really appreciate the game."

She pressed a palm to her forehead. "Oh my goodness, what have I started."

* * *

Inside the duffel bag were a Chicago Cubs kid's jacket, two T-shirts, a portable speaker, a pair of Cubs pajama pants, Cubs socks and two pairs of ear buds. Miles was going to have to take his old buddy out for dinner one night for this one. Kyla was beside herself when she saw all the goodies. She smiled so big it made Miles's day. He loved to see her smile, and he loved being the one to cause that smile.

They left Wrigley Field and strolled down Chicago's famous Magnificent Mile. The Sunday evening crowd had thinned out and the stores would be closing soon. He was scheduled to attend a fund-raising event Monday night, and since he'd talked her into staying, he wanted her to go with him.

As they walked into Bloomingdale's he brought it up. "Tomorrow night I'll be attending a charity event for the UNCF. It's black tie, and I want you to go with me."

Kyla's jaw dropped, and she shook her head. "Miles, I can't. I didn't bring an appropriate dress for that."

He laughed. "Don't worry, we'll find you something today."

She looked around. "Maybe tomorrow we can go someplace else."

He took her hand. "Come on. Let's find you a dress."

It took her over an hour to pick out a dress and a pair of shoes. Afterward, he surprised her by taking her to dinner at one of Chicago's famous farm-to-table restaurants.

By the time they arrived back at his condo for the evening, he just wanted a shower and his bed.

As Miles strolled through the lobby with her suitcase and garment bag, the doorman greeted Kyla with a big smile. He walked over to call the elevator for Miles, since he had his hands full.

"Sir, is there anything I can get you this evening?" he asked as they waited on the elevator.

"No, thanks, we're fine." And then an idea came to him. "Wait a minute, there is something... Would you order me a bottle of champagne and some strawberries?"

The doorman smiled. "Yes, sir. I'll bring them up as soon as they arrive."

"Thank you." The elevator doors swung open, and Miles stood back as Kyla entered.

She crossed her arms and leaned against the elevator wall the minute the door closed. "So is that something you do often?" she asked.

Miles turned to her. "What?"

"The champagne and strawberries. You didn't even have to tell him where to go or what to get. It sounded rather routine to me."

He shrugged. "There's a specialty store around the corner that I order food from occasionally. It's not a problem."

"No, it didn't sound like it would be a problem. More like something he's used to doing for you."

Miles smiled and shook his head. "It's not a routine of mine, just something I thought would be a nice way to cap off the evening."

The elevator stopped and the doors swooshed open. He backed away.

"After you, my dear," he said as Kyla walked out past him.

She smiled. "You're such a gentleman."

"Yeah, I know. My mama taught me well," he replied.

Once inside, he deposited her belongings in his guest room. Exhausted, they both lounged on the sofa to unwind. It was big enough for him to sit back and pull her between his legs. Miles held her in his arms while they watched a little television. The Kyla he'd experienced this weekend was different from the teacher Kyla from the farm. This

Kyla was sexier, yet she was the same down-to-earth, loving woman he'd fallen for weeks ago. However, he could tell she had something on her mind. She hadn't said much since they left Wrigley Field.

Minutes later, when the doorbell rang, it woke them both. Miles was surprised to realize he'd fallen asleep. He went to answer the door, while Kyla went into the guest room to freshen up.

His doorman held up a small shopping bag from one of the boutique grocers down the street. "Your champagne and strawberries, sir. They placed it on your account."

Miles smiled and took the bag. "Right on time. I appreciate this."

"You're welcome."

Miles tipped his doorman before closing the door. He took everything into the kitchen. The champagne and strawberries were already chilled, so he placed them in the refrigerator to keep them that way until after his shower.

When he emerged, he found Kyla in the living room sitting on the sofa with her feet tucked under her, watching a movie. His body woke up at the sight of her. She'd showered and changed into a pair of shorts and a tank top with Garden Ninja inscribed on the front. Her hair was pulled up into a high ponytail, which made her neck look longer and added to the gracefulness of her profile.

"Well, don't you look refreshed," he said as he crossed the room.

"Miles, I need to ask you something."

He continued into the room joining her on the sofa. "What's on your mind?" he asked, reaching out to stroke her ponytail.

"How many women have you toured the clubhouse with before, and brought up here for a nightcap?"

He let out a deep breath. "I noticed your face when Captain mentioned my *friends*. He was referring to Glenda,

Brandon, and possibly my sister. I gave her a tour when she came up for a game once. He didn't mean girlfriends if that's what you're thinking."

"What I'm thinking is you told me the Miles from the tabloids was you a long time ago. But I'm not so sure now. I'm starting to feel like that Miles is still in operation and I'm the latest casualty."

He sat straight up and gave her his undivided attention. "Kyla, if I was still involved with anybody I would not have invited you here. And I don't think you would have accepted my invitation to move out of the hotel if you felt that way."

She slowly shook her head.

"So, whatever is causing doubt to creep into your head, push it away. You have to trust that I'm who I say I am."

She sighed.

He sat back on the sofa and took a deep breath. This was not the way he wanted the evening to end. "So can we spend some time watching a little television and enjoying the champagne?"

"I suppose so."

"Kyla I want you to be comfortable while you're here. Little things like this, I want you to discuss them with me. Always let me know how you feel."

"Okay, something else that's on my mind. When's Brandon coming back?" Kyla asked.

"Tomorrow some time. Why?"

"Oh, I just wondered. What do you think he'll say when he finds out I'm staying here instead of the hotel?"

He sat up until he was on the edge of the sofa. "This is my condo, not Brandon's. Besides, I think he'll be happy to see you again." He stood up, and leaned down to kiss the tip of her nose.

"I hope so. I wouldn't want to cause a rift between you two by being here."

"You don't have to worry about that. As a matter of fact, you don't have to worry about anything." He turned around and headed for the kitchen. He pulled the champagne and strawberries out of the refrigerator. While he worked in the kitchen, she took the remote and found a rerun of the Country Music Awards show playing on cable.

Miles frowned first, then smiled as he joined her with two champagne flutes and a bowl of strawberries. She took the flutes while he set the berries on the table. "So, this is what we're watching?" he asked. Her selection didn't exactly go with his treat of choice for the evening.

"Do you mind?" she asked with a glow in her eyes.

He wiggled his brows. He wasn't a country music fan like she was. But maybe he'd discover some music he liked. "Enjoy yourself, baby."

They sat back and watched. He found it more enjoyable than he thought he would. When he fed her strawberries, she sucked the sweet fruit—along with his fingers—into her mouth. Throughout the rest of the show they enjoyed the berries, the champagne and each other's lips.

Miles didn't care what was on the television. His only interest was in the woman sitting between his thighs. She had her long legs stretched out on his sofa and her body pressed against his penis, just begging for his attention. He reached down and slid the band from her ponytail, wanting to see her hair cascading around her shoulders. She turned around and looked up into his eyes, and he couldn't help but run his hands through her hair.

She scooted up until their lips met and he tasted the sweet berries on her lips and then inside her warm mouth. His hands slid around her waist and under her tank top, caressing her firm nipples through her lacy bra. He sat up and swung his legs off the sofa, bringing her with him as she sat facing him and wrapped her legs around him. All of the exhaustion from earlier left his body and he reached around her back and unsnapped her bra, freeing her soft breasts into the palms of his hands. Country music cried from the television while Kyla moaned into his mouth.

She straddled him, moving her hips up closer and closer until she was directly over his penis, driving him crazy. He pulled the ends of her tank up and over her raised arms, along with her bra, tossing them to the floor. Last night he'd gotten a taste of her, but tonight he wanted to feast. She arched her back, and her perfect nipples called out to him. He delicately placed his lips over one and licked with slow, soft strokes. She was coming unglued at his touch. She reached down and tugged on his T-shirt until he leaned forward to let her pull it up and over his head. Their bodies came together, and Miles buried his face in her neck. She smelled like fresh flowers and love, if it had a smell.

"Woman, what are you doing to me?" he asked, as he held onto her working hips. He was fully erect now and didn't think he could take much more of this. He rested his head back on the sofa and slid farther down.

She leaned forward, sitting directly on top of him, now nibbling at his neck. Her hair fell across his chest and he tried to take a deep breath. "You're making it hard for me to breathe," he gasped.

She slowed down and sat up, pulling her hair to one side. "You started this by plying me with alcohol and strawberries." She traced his lips with her finger. "You knew what you were doing."

He grinned and reached out with both hands, filling his palms with her breasts, caressing them. "You checked out of the hotel and moved in here." He leaned forward and kissed a nipple. "You knew exactly what you were doing, too," he countered.

Her mouth formed a perfect circle, and he thought he'd lose his mind.

"Why, Mr. Parker, are you insinuating that I knew we

would end up making wild passionate love all night if I stayed here?" she asked in a teasing voice, while grinding deeper into him.

He burst out laughing and threw his head back again. Since arriving in Chicago, he'd seen a side of her he'd never thought existed. "Man, I never know what to expect from you anymore. And this sexy vixen Kyla? I love her."

She giggled before leaning forward and licking his nipple. "The condoms are in the bedroom," he said in a hoarse voice he barely recognized himself. He knew she'd heard him, but she moved from one nipple to the other and began to suck. He squeezed his ass cheeks together and gripped her hips to keep them from moving. He bit his lip so hard he thought he tasted blood. That was it! He couldn't take it any longer. Before he exploded, he held her by the arms and removed her from his lap, setting her next to him on the sofa. Her hair was all tousled, making her look hot as hell. She fell back, taking deep breaths.

He stood up, adjusting the tent in his pants. She looked so hot and seductive, he wanted to take her right there on the sofa, but he sucked it up and reached down for her hand. "Come on. I've got something to show you in the bedroom."

She stood up, grinning. "I'll bet you do."

The minute she walked in front of him, he reached down and smacked her on the ass. She jumped and glanced back at him with a sultry smile on her face. "Don't start nothing you can't finish."

With those words, his whole body ached to finish what they'd started.

Chapter 17

Kyla's prediction had been correct. They spent Sunday night making love until Miles practically fell into a coma, he slept so soundly. Monday morning came around too soon. He took the day off, wanting to spend as much time with Kyla as he could. While she soaked in his bathtub, he cooked the only meal he was any good at, breakfast. He carried a tray of turkey bacon, scrambled eggs, toast and orange juice down the hall, stopping at the bathroom door. Balancing everything on one hand, he knocked on the door.

"Come in," she called out in a voice that sounded like a woman in love.

Smiling, Miles turned the knob and then grabbed the tray before it tilted over. He entered the bathroom and walked over to the tub. She sat in a pool of bubbles with her hair piled on top of her head. "I thought you could use a little nourishment after last night," he said, and draped the tray over the edge of the tub.

"You made all this for me?" she asked, squeezing the washcloth in her hand.

He nodded. "See what you got me doing. And I didn't burn the toast."

She ate her breakfast while he went back to the kitchen to clean up the disaster area before she finished.

Before lunch, in preparation for the United Negro College Fund Fundraising Gala later that night, Kyla tried on her dress for him. His jaw dropped at the sight of her slim frame in the cream-colored off-the-shoulder dress with small ruffles and lace-up arm details. The dress, with a slit up one thigh, gave her a chic, polished look. She held up her hair, asking him if she should wear it up or down.

Miles walked over and removed her hand, allowing her hair to fall. "Which way do you think I like it?" he asked, before wrapping his arm around her waist.

She placed a palm on his chest. "If you mess up this dress before I have a chance to wear it, I'll never forgive you."

"Then I think you'd better take it off," he said, letting go, but not before giving her a quick kiss on the lips. "Because something about you and this look right here is really turning me on. I'm not sure if we'll make the fundraiser." Miles licked his lips, thinking about all the things he wanted to do to her.

As luck would have it, Brandon returned home before Miles and Kyla could get into anything. Over lunch Brandon filled them in on his weekend.

"Miles I know you want me to come work with you after graduation, but I've got some great news."

Miles glanced at Kyla afraid of what his little brother was about to say. Then nodded for Brandon to continue.

"I might be headed to London on a paid internship."

"London! Why London?" Miles asked.

"Well, my buddy's dad wants to talk to me about the

internship. It will be a chance to get some international experience. Plus, I met a girl from there this week."

Miles sat back and crossed his arms. "So what you're really telling me is you met a girl and you want to move to London."

Brandon shrugged. "Something like that, yeah."

"I see that a week on the farm wasn't enough." Glenda teased Miles as he stood at the bar waiting on Kyla's drink. Every year, Parker Edmunds purchased a table for the gala, happy to give their support to the UNCF's efforts. Glenda wore a black gown with a plunging neckline and front split to show off her supermodel body for her date, Quan.

Miles took a sip of his drink before responding. "A month wouldn't have been enough."

Glenda turned around with her back to the bar, finding Kyla across the room. "She's beautiful and sweet, and she's all about organic farming. Have you discussed your differences?"

He shook his head. "I'm sure we'll find some common ground. I don't have anything against organic farming, you know that. It's just not how I make my money."

"But I'm willing to bet it's her life. And Miles, most organic farmers are very passionate about what they do."

"Oh, she's passionate all right, about everything she does. But the farm is run by her cousins. She's just working there until she gets her PhD."

Glenda shrugged. "So what? I'm sure she's not going to give up her nonprofit work once she gets her degree. She's going to protest against everything you do. Everything *we* do. And from what I've seen so far, she can be very persuasive."

Miles looked at Kyla, standing several feet away talking to a group of women who worked on the UNCF scholarship fund. Glenda was right about one thing: organic food was Kyla's life. She planned on spreading her hands-on workshops all over the state of Kentucky, which he could wholeheartedly support. But could she also support him in his efforts to rid the world of hunger in his way?

Kyla left Chicago Wednesday afternoon, and returned to her life in Danville, Kentucky. She spent the next week missing Miles, having to settle for brief phone calls and text messages. Each morning she woke happy that another day had passed, shortening the time she'd be away from him. She couldn't wait for him to return to Lexington over the weekend. She was debating whether she'd travel up to see him or whether he'd come down to see her, but either way, he promised they'd see each other. While she worked, images of Miles danced in her head: Miles shirtless, Miles laughing, Miles lying naked next to her and Miles making love to her. But the one image that was etched in her brain was that of Miles admitting he'd broken his vow because he found in her the woman he wanted to spend the rest of his life with.

The bright sunshine, the heat and the sweat rolling down Kyla's back all reminded her that her fantasy weekend was over. She didn't know what would happen to her and Miles now, but she was glad to be back on familiar territory. She'd missed the morning truck rides, the guests eager to hit the fields to start collecting their dinner and her sidekick, Kevin.

Kyla jumped when the truck door slammed and Kevin walked back toward her. "Is everything okay?" she asked, while shoving empty baskets under the seats of the truck bed.

"Women. I'll never understand them," Kevin replied, shaking his head.

"So, what did you do?" she asked, knowing Kevin.

He ran his hand through his hair. "I went out with some

friends, and somebody told her they saw me with another woman. Who's she gonna believe, me or some fool she don't know?"

"Maybe you need to sit down face-to-face instead of having it out over the phone."

"Yeah, well, that's what I've been trying to do. She won't see me."

"Don't give up. If you two are meant to be, it'll work out." Before she went to check and see if any of the guests needed help, she walked over and stood next to Kevin.

"Well, look at you, giving out relationship advice."

Kyla waved him off.

"Your weekend must have went better than you're letting on, considering you extended it and everything."

She shrugged. "I had a great time with a great guy."

"Yeah, so I see. What's that on your face?" He pointed at her cheeks.

Kyla wiped at the sides of her mouth. "I don't feel anything. Do you still see it?"

"Yeah. It's a glow, and it's all over."

She lowered her hand and punched him in the arm. "I'm gonna hurt you."

"No, seriously. I noticed it when you came out the back door this morning." He threw his hands up and backed up. "That's all I'm saying."

Kyla narrowed her eyes at him and looked for something to throw as he kept backing up.

During the ride back to the farm, one of the couples led the group in song. It was shaping up to be a beautiful day. When Kyla walked into the house, Tayler informed her there was a gentleman in the library waiting to talk to her.

"Who is he?" Kyla asked.

Tayler widened her lips and shrugged. "I don't know. He won't say."

"Okay." Kyla stopped in the bathroom first to wash

her hands, then opened the door that separated the family quarters from the rest of the house. In the library, a slender white man stood by the bookshelf looking at the collection of guests' photographs. He turned around when he heard her enter.

"Hello, I'm Kyla Coleman. Are you waiting for me?"

He smiled and crossed the room, offering his hand. "Yes, Ms. Coleman, my name's Dave Johnson, and if you have a few minutes I'd like to speak to you about the property on Mansell Road in Nicholasville."

Kyla's back straightened. That's where her parents lived. "What about it?" she asked, unable to keep the defensive tone from her voice.

He looked around. "Do you mind if we sit down?"

She shook her head. "No, have a seat." The hair on the nape of her neck stood up, and she knew this could not be good news.

He sat on one end of the sofa while Kyla sat on the other. He reached down for a portfolio she hadn't seen propped next to the sofa and pulled out some papers.

"I've just come from the property after making an offer to purchase for a client of mine. As you know, the property is in preforeclosure due to back taxes and overdue loans." He glanced down at his paper. "The property is deeded to Paula Montgomery." Then he looked back up at Kyla. "I believe that's your mother's maiden name."

Kyla sat back deep into the sofa and looked at this skinny man with slicked-back black hair and silver wire-rimmed glasses, and wondered who the hell he was. She nodded. "What did you say your name was, again?"

He reached into his jacket pocket and produced a business card. "Dave Johnson, investment Realtor for The Lucas Group."

She studied the card a couple of seconds, then looked up. "Paula Montgomery is my mother's maiden name, yes.

But, I think somebody's made a mistake. The property is not in foreclosure."

He took a deep breath. "No, not yet. It's in preforeclosure."

She sat up. "Who told you that? It's not in pre- or any other type of foreclosure, and it's certainly not for sale."

Mr. Johnson cleared his throat. "Hmmm…we've sent several letters and postcards, and I visited Mr. Ernie Coleman this morning when I didn't get a response to any of the correspondence. I'm afraid he was not ready to listen to my offer."

She crossed her arms. "So, what makes you think I want to hear anything you have to say?"

He cleared his throat. "Yes, well, after I spoke with my client relaying your father's response, he suggested I come speak to you. He said you would understand the—"

"Wait a minute, who is your client?" she snapped. She'd had just about enough of this guy, who was probably trying to trick her parents out of their land. Where was Gavin? He should be discussing this with him.

"The Lucas Group is representing Parker Edmunds."

Kyla gasped and tilted her head. She could not have heard him right. "Miles Parker?" she asked for clarification.

"Yes, he suggested I pay you a visit. We're hoping you can help us."

The room began to spin, and Kyla's body weakened. She was at a loss for words. The sensation of things moving too quickly to process took over her body. Miles wouldn't do this to her! Her heart was pounding as she looked up at this errand boy. "Would you please leave?" she asked with a tremor in her voice.

"Do you think you'll—"

"GET OUT!" she yelled.

Chapter 18

Kyla spent the rest of Friday catching up on her work. Whatever someone needed help with, she was there. She needed something to keep her mind off her visitor earlier. She didn't believe a word he'd said. If there was trouble at home, Tracee would have told her. Besides, she told herself there was no way her family was about to lose their farm. Her mother's family owned other land in Nicholasville, and he must have mistaken the properties.

Miles hadn't called her all day long, and after what her visitor said, she wasn't going to call him. Since she'd left Chicago they'd spoken almost every day, so she found it strange that he hadn't called today.

Saturday morning's truck ride was a welcome diversion. The guests always kept her busy. For a couple of hours, at least, she was able to get her mind off Miles and her visitor. However, after she returned to the B and B, the thoughts resurfaced. Tracee hadn't been home last night, and she'd taken the morning off to volunteer with a church program, so Kyla couldn't talk to her. When Corra asked her to cover the gift shop while she ran into town, Kyla eagerly did so.

Now that people were driving up to the B and B not only as guests, but as patrons of the U-pick store and Rooted Beginnings workshops, business in the gift shop had picked up. Corra practically ran things herself, so whenever Kyla had the time, she helped out as much as she could. Today she decided to do some restocking while Corra was out. In the back room, an endless supply of whatnots in boxes lined the shelves. Kyla took stock of what they were low on and began opening boxes.

A few minutes into her job, the bell over the door jingled. She had a customer. "I'll be right with you," she called out before stopping what she was doing and walking out to be of assistance.

Miles stood inside the door looking around, and her heart skipped a beat. He'd gotten a haircut since Chicago, and he looked so handsome. She hesitated before running over to greet him. Why hadn't he called first?

He smiled the minute he laid eyes on her. "Hey, how you doin'?"

They walked across the floor to greet each other, and she noticed a slight hesitation on his part, as well.

"I'm fine. How did you know I was in here?" she asked.

Miles rocked back on his heels before leaning in for a forehead kiss. She pulled back slightly from the kiss, a little leery of him right now.

"Tayler told me. I went up to the house first. She said you were covering for your cousin." He took a step closer and pulled her back into his embrace. "What's wrong, didn't you miss me?" he asked, kissing her on the neck when she looked away.

Kyla moved out of his arms again and walked over behind the cash register, pretending she had something to do. "Why didn't you call or text to let me know you were coming?"

He followed her, standing on the other side of the counter. "I told you I'd see you this weekend. I flew in yesterday morning, but I had so much to do I couldn't get away."

She nodded. "Like sending some real estate guy over here hoping I'd help you out?" she asked, as she picked up a pencil and tapped it against the counter. She knew the look she gave him made him uncomfortable, and she was happy about that right now.

Miles drew his lips into a straight line and took a deep breath. "He told me you asked him to leave," he said, frowning.

"So, you did send him to talk to me?" She flipped the pencil over, and it landed on the floor. Her stomach fluttered at the same time, and she blocked it out.

"I did," he said with confidence. "He was just doing his job, and I thought if he explained it to you, you might be able to explain it to your father."

He looked so calm, standing there telling her he wanted to take her family's land. She couldn't believe it. "I think you need to start from the beginning and tell me what this is about. Is that the land Glenda mentioned looking at in Nicholasville?" she asked in an uncertain tone.

He nodded. "Yeah, we've been looking to purchase some property south of Lexington, and Glenda found this preforeclosure over a month ago. But the deed wasn't under Coleman, so I had no idea your parents lived there. It was just another business deal. But I've never been comfortable with foreclosures, so I had my advisor dig around and get me some information on the owners. I wanted to make sure I wasn't putting anyone out in the street. Just last week I learned the occupants were your parents."

Kyla shook her head. "I don't believe you. Like I told

your real estate guy, if my parents were losing their home, I think I would know."

He leaned against the counter palms down and looked genuinely concerned. "Kyla, I'm sorry. I hate to be the one to break it to you."

She crossed her arms. "Even if it were true, you didn't say anything to me once you discovered it. We've spoken since last week."

"I know. I thought you might be embarrassed if I brought it up, although you shouldn't be. We've sent cards to your father offering to purchase the land. But he's never replied."

She kept shaking her head. "My family is not moving, nor is their land for sale. You must have mixed something up." She heard her own voice rise several octaves, and a heavy feeling weighed on her chest.

Miles came around the counter closer to Kyla. She wanted him to stop. She didn't want him to touch her.

He reached out and held her by the arms. "Kyla, you think the whole time we were looking at the land we knew it belonged to your family? That I knew your mother and father lived on that land and I didn't say anything to you?"

She nodded. "You want me to talk them into selling, don't you?"

He took a deep breath. "They're about to lose the land, Kyla. If you don't believe me, call them and find out for yourself. I'm surprised you didn't already know."

"Let me ask you something." Now things were starting to click for her.

He lowered his arms. "Sure. Anything."

"Did you know when we were in Chicago?"

He shook his head. "No, of course not. That would have been the perfect time to discuss it. Believe me, I had no malicious intentions. The minute I found out, I sat down with my team and we drafted the best offer my company could make. Trust me, I wouldn't do anything to hurt you or your family."

"But you sent someone to talk to my family without saying a word to me."

He sighed. "My business is with the property owners. We had to approach them first."

She placed both hands on her hips. "Yeah, how did that go?"

"According to the Realtor, not so well. But I don't believe he was given a chance to give his pitch. That's why, when he called me, I suggested he speak to you. I figured once you saw what a good deal it was, you'd be able to persuade them to sell, and we'd talk then. We're working against the clock. If they don't act soon, they'll lose everything."

She couldn't believe all of this and started to feel a little betrayed by Miles.

He lowered his voice. "Kyla, you need to sit down and have a talk with your parents. I only know what was in the preforeclosure documents. But if it's gotten this far, things are bad. And I'm not the enemy."

Kyla's head was spinning. The fact that Miles possibly knew more about her family's finances than she did hurt and upset her. She hadn't been home in a month, but the last time she was there, everything appeared to be okay. Gavin hadn't mentioned anything to her about the family struggling to pay the bills, and neither had Tracee, for that matter. If it was true, she wondered if her siblings knew—or had they been kept in the dark, as well?

The bell over the door jingled, and it couldn't have been at a worse time. Kyla glanced that way to see a young woman walk in, taking off her sunglasses. Miles crossed the room and greeted her at the door.

"I'm sorry, but can we ask you to come back in just a few minutes? We need to close for a second to cash out the register." With a smile on his face, he held the woman by her elbow as she turned around. She looked slightly confused, but agreed to come back.

"Thank you so much," Miles said as he closed the door behind her and flipped over the Open sign to read Closed.

Kyla couldn't help but think back to the days of Miles shadowing her. He'd asked a lot of questions. She'd told him she was from Nicholasville, but he never asked her anything about her family. Maybe because he already knew. Maybe she was the real reason he'd checked into the B and B in the first place.

Had he played her this whole time? Had he had ulterior motives from the moment he met her at the Hunger Day conference? He'd known exactly how to get to her. He'd known how much she wanted to go to the Global Summit, and he'd just happened to have an extra ticket. He hadn't told her about the fundraiser, so he'd had a reason to take her shopping and buy her a dress. Was it all to entice her into doing whatever he wanted? She'd read that he was smooth, and he'd asked her not to believe everything she read. Well, maybe the papers were right about one thing. Maybe Miles Parker was a master charmer.

Miles walked back up to the counter. "I'm going up to the house to speak to Rollin for a minute. Do you want to go grab something to eat after you finish here?"

Her eyes widened at the possibility of him sharing all this information with Rollin.

Miles shook his head. "I haven't said anything to anybody."

And how long would that last? She needed to talk to her family before the rumor mill started. "No, you go ahead. I have work to do."

Miles looked at her, drumming his fingers on the counter. "You know I drove all the way down here to see you?"

She moved away from the register and crossed her arms.

"To talk to me, you mean. To pick up where your Realtor failed. Isn't that really why you *drove all the way* down here?" The ride had taken him an hour, if that long.

"I wanted to explain the situation to you, yes, but that's not why I'm here. I'm here because I miss you and I wanted to see you again."

"Well, you've seen me," she replied with a curt smile.

"I don't know what's rattling around in that pretty little head of yours, but I need you to understand something. When I said you were the one for me, I meant it. I came to spend some time with you. I want us to get to know each other better."

"I think I know you about as well as I want to. You're good. You just charm the pants off any woman you want. Now you seduce people for the betterment of your company. You and Glenda are probably just alike. I bet she's seducing Quan so he'll invest in your business in some way. I see how you like to mix business with pleasure."

"Stop it, Kyla! Where is all of this coming from? What has gotten into you?"

"You're not going to take my family's land and spread your pesticides all over it, ruining what they've spent years working on. That land is how they make their money. If they lose the farm, where will they go? Farming is my family's life."

Miles dropped his shoulders and let out a deep sigh. He looked up at Kyla, slowly shaking his head.

Tracee had warned her about Miles. She'd said he was far more experienced than Kyla was, but Kyla hadn't taken into account how slick he could be.

Miles started talking again, slower this time. "Kyla, the foreclosure is not going away unless your family comes up with some money. They stand to lose everything to the bank. I may be their only solution. My offer to purchase the land gives them enough to pay off the debt and move to another home or a smaller farm. Whatever they chose to do with it is their business, but their credit won't be ruined."

"How can I believe you, Miles?"

"Don't believe me. Pick up the phone and call your parents."

"My father's a proud man. He keeps things close to his chest."

"Then maybe you need to go see him in person. Talk everything over with them. I have no desire to hurt your family in any way."

She looked away from him and nodded. She knew there was a chip on her shoulder the size of Mount Rushmore, but she couldn't help it.

"Now, can we talk about us?" Miles asked.

Kyla shook her head and walked over to open the gift shop door. "There's nothing to talk about. I'm sorry, but I'm gonna have to ask you to leave." She thrust up her chin, trying to look brave, but inside, her body was broken and her heart hurt. She couldn't shake the feeling that she'd been had by a jock, yet again.

"Well, look who's back in town!"

Kyla turned her head as Corra walked in, smiling up at Miles.

"Hi Corra, it's good to see you again. I came down to spend some time with Kyla, but—"

"But I'm kind of busy today, so he was on his way out." Kyla cut him off before he shared any details of their conversation with Corra. It irritated her that he was still standing there. Her heartbeat pounded in her chest and heat flushed through her body while she forced the corners of her lips up into something that resembled a smile.

Miles said goodbye and Kyla closed the door behind him.

Chapter 19

After Miles left, Corra kept asking if everything was okay. Kyla told her yes, but she knew Corra was no fool, and she'd detected that something had happened between Kyla and Miles.

"So, are you and Miles getting together tonight?" Corra asked.

"No. We aren't. He just stopped by to say hello. I've got a ton of work to do today."

Corra walked over to the door and flipped the sign to Open. "How did that get turned around?"

Explaining that would mean she had to explain Miles's presence, so Kyla shook her head. "I don't know, maybe I accidently did it when I opened the door to let you in."

"Well, if you don't have anywhere to run off to, let's look over the details for the potluck scheduled for the end of the month." Corra walked behind the counter and pulled out a three-ring binder, then gestured to Kyla. "Come on, pull up a stool and let's have a look."

Kyla took a deep breath before joining her cousin. She wasn't about to leave the gift shop with Miles still on the property. She didn't want to bump into him on his way out. What she needed to do was get her parents on the phone, or find Gavin. If anything Miles said was true, Gavin would know.

As she pulled one of the stools from the end of the counter next to Corra, she asked, "Have you seen Tracee?"

"Not since this morning. She said something about meeting a friend for lunch. She didn't say where, but I doubt she's gone too far."

Kyla listened to Corra walk through the details of the community potluck, wanting her opinion before presenting it to the families involved. She tried to focus, but her mind was elsewhere. Periodically, she glanced out the window to see if Miles's SUV was still parked in the lot—it was.

"So, you wanna tell me what's going on?" Corra finally said.

Kyla averted her cousin's gaze and shook her head. "Nothing."

Corra cleared her throat. "Okay, so you don't want to talk. I'm not surprised. But Kyla, you flew to Chicago and spent five days with Miles, then returned happy as a schoolgirl after her first kiss. Now he comes to see you and you don't look happy at all. You practically slammed the door on him when he walked out of here."

Kyla bit the inside of her cheek and glanced up at Corra.

"Yeah, honey, I don't miss a thing. What did he say to upset you?"

"I'd rather not talk about it," Kyla said.

"Well, you need to talk to somebody. Tayler told me about you moping around here yesterday, and then Miles shows up today. You know we're here for you, no matter what. If he did something wrong, let us know. The Coleman women will be all over him before he knows what's going on." Corra held her fist up.

Kyla laughed at Corra's fighting stance, as if she'd be ready to fight Miles if she had to. "I appreciate that cuz, you know I do, but Miles has always been a perfect gentleman."

Corra threw her hands up. "Okay, so if you don't want to talk about it, you don't have to. I just want you to know I'm here for you, and I know how to keep my mouth shut."

Kyla thought about it for a minute while Corra flipped the potluck binder closed. Maybe she could use Corra's help if what Miles said was true. Maybe they'd need a lawyer, and Chris would definitely be able to suggest somebody good.

She decided to confide in her cousin. "Corra, Miles came by to give me some disturbing news. But promise me you'll keep this between us right now?"

Corra's eyes widened. "I promise."

So Kyla told her everything.

As Kyla hurried out of the gift shop and up to the house, she pulled out her cell phone and dialed first her parents, and then Gavin without getting an answer. On the way, she noticed Miles's SUV was gone. After giving Corra most of the details of her conversation with Miles, Corra suggested Kyla get in touch with her family right away. Corra also assured Kyla that she could count on Corra and Chris to help in any way they were needed.

Kyla tried Tracee next, and almost jumped for joy when she answered her phone.

"Hey girl, hold on," Tracee said.

Kyla entered the house through the back door and made her way to her room as Tracee returned to the line.

"Okay, what's up? I had to put my earbuds in."

"What do you know about Momma and Daddy possibly losing the farm?"

Tracee let out a deep sigh. "Who've you been talking to?"

Kyla didn't want her to know Miles was that deep into their family business. "I just heard something. Tell me what you know."

After a brief hesitation, Tracee said, "We need to talk. I'm not coming back to the B and B today, and I'm finished here so I'm going home. Drop by as soon as you finish work."

Kyla paced around her bedroom floor. "Okay. Just tell me, is it bad news or not?"

"We'll talk when I see you. I'll call Gavin, too, because the three of us need to talk before you talk to mama or daddy."

Kyla shook her head. Anytime somebody said *we need to talk* it wasn't good news. She agreed to meet Tracee later and hung up. She tossed her cell phone across the bed and sat on the end with her forehead in her hands. She had a feeling this was going to be more serious than she'd anticipated.

A couple of hours later, Tracee opened the front door before Kyla could knock. "I saw you pull up," she explained, holding the door open.

Kyla took a deep breath as she walked in. Tracee's face was all made up, and her hair was done up into a tasteful bun. If it hadn't been for the maxi dress and sandals, Kyla would say she looked like she was prepared for a job interview.

"Come on in here. I called Gavin, and he'll call us back when he's free."

Kyla followed Tracee into her cozy, elegantly decorated kitchen. Two glasses and a bottle of white wine sat on the counter, next to a plate of brownies. "You're always baking. I'm surprised you don't weigh a ton," Kyla said as she reached over to sample a brownie.

Tracee walked over and pulled the bottle opener from a drawer. "Baking is my job, and I don't eat everything I bake. That's why I set these out here for you. Help yourself."

Silence filled the room while Kyla ate her brownie. Tracee poured two glasses of wine and joined her at the table. Kyla took a deep breath, ready to hear the worst.

"So, you heard about the foreclosure?" Tracee asked.

Kyla's hand flew to her chest. "Is it a done deal?"

Tracee took a sip from her glass. "No, not yet."

Kyla leaned back in her seat and picked up her wine. She took a couple of sips before putting the glass down. "So, how did this happen, and how come nobody told me about it? I felt like a fool when I found out."

Tracee swirled the wine around in her glass. "I found out from Gavin that a couple of months ago Daddy started missing mortgage payments. Things had been slow for quite a while. I had no idea, because every time I went home, things looked fine. Momma and Daddy are good at keeping up appearances."

"So things are slow. That shouldn't be a big enough deal to cause them to lose everything."

Tracee shrugged. "There's more to it. Gavin should—"

The house phone rang. Tracee jumped up. "That's probably him now." She walked over to pick up the cordless from the counter.

Kyla massaged her forehead, thinking about all the stuff she'd said to Miles. She'd wanted so bad for him to be wrong.

"Okay, Gavin, tell Kyla what you told me." Tracee placed the phone on speaker and set it in between them on the table.

"Hey, Gavin," Kyla greeted him.

"Hey, sis. So, who told you?"

Kyla stared at the phone, still not wanting to give up Miles's name. She looked up at Tracee, who gave her a questioning look, waiting for her answer also. She leaned forward, placing her forearms on the table. "An investment Realtor for Parker Edmunds came by the farm on Saturday asking me if I'd talk to Daddy. They want to purchase the farm instead of letting it go into foreclosure."

"Yeah, that's who came by here. Unfortunately, I wasn't here at the time, and the old man is still somewhat in denial about the whole situation."

"Gavin, what happened?" Kyla asked.

"A lot of things. A couple of years ago we expected large growth, so Daddy took out a loan for some new machinery. That growth never happened, but loans came due, and you name it. We had to do whatever we could to survive."

"So, they don't have any other money in the bank?" Kyla asked, knowing the answer but reaching for anything.

"Kyla, at times we can't even pay the guys who help us out. We've exhausted every resource there is. And I have my family to think about. I've been thinking about getting out of the farming business and doing something else to support my family. Right now, we're living off of Donna's income. I couldn't even afford to send the girls to camp this summer, and forget a vacation."

Kyla's chin dipped to her chest. She was afraid of this. "How's Mom holding up?"

"As well as can be expected. You need to come see her. Both of you need to come. She's been pretending everything is okay for so long. I think she's just trying to keep Daddy from getting depressed. Not that he isn't already."

Tracee leaned into the phone. "Since the land came from Momma's side of the family, have you spoken to any of her brothers?"

Gavin snorted into the phone. "Are you kidding? Only Uncle Calvin has any land left, and he's been selling off acres a little at a time."

"Aren't there any government subsidies, loans or anything they can get?" Desperation coated Kyla's words. She reached for her wine glass. "Maybe somebody else in the area would want to buy them out."

"Like I told Tracee, we've already tried everything, and there's nothing. We can't even refinance. Before he purchased the new machinery I'd suggested he consider selling and getting out. But he wanted to give it a little longer. He had faith things would turn around."

Kyla and Tracee sat staring at each other, Kyla with tears in her eyes. Memories of the huge backyard where the three of them used to play ran through her mind. Her mother used to hang the laundry on lines out back, and they'd run around the clothes, hitting them with baseball bats until her mother ran them off.

"Unless the two of you want to move back home and help out? Don't even answer that, I was being facetious. Even your help couldn't save us. But you do need to ride up for a visit. We'll all sit down and talk. That guy left some papers around somewhere."

"Gavin, we can talk about it, but we don't have to take their offer," Kyla said.

"Have you even seen Parker Edmunds's offer?"

"No, but…"

"Gavin," Tracee butted in. "Miles Parker's the owner of Parker Edmunds, and that's the guy who invited Kyla to the Global Summit last week."

"No shit! So, you know this guy, Kyla?"

She frowned and squished up her nose at Tracee for telling Gavin about her relationship with Miles. Her sister shrugged as if she'd done nothing wrong. After explaining to Gavin how she knew Miles, and why she didn't trust his offer, she received nothing but silence from either sibling.

"Hello," she said into the speakerphone.

"Yeah, I'm here. I heard you, but it doesn't make sense. Why plot to take the land when he can just wait for it to go into foreclosure and possibly get it cheaper?"

"Booyah!" Tracee shouted, and pumped her fist one time.

Kyla jumped.

Tracee leaned in closer to the phone. "That's exactly what I'm thinking. I mean, I don't know a lot about foreclosures, but wouldn't he then be responsible for the unpaid taxes and loans?"

"That's right," Gavin confirmed. "But if he purchases the property in preforeclosure, we take care of all the debt connected to the house. He also avoids a bidding war if somebody else wants it."

Tracee kept nodding in agreement with Gavin.

"But where are all you guys gonna live?" Kyla asked.

He snorted. "Someplace with a shower, a dishwasher and a two-car garage. Kyla, do you know how old this place is? You're staying over there with Rollin and Tayler with all their modern conveniences, and Tracee has her townhouse. I'm the one stuck fixing all this old shit up all the time. I think Mama would be happy to leave."

"I can't imagine them living anyplace else," Kyla said.

"Well, we have about two months before the foreclosure. We haven't listed the property for sale because Daddy doesn't want to, but we have to do something before the foreclosure becomes public knowledge. You know how proud the old man is. That would kill him."

Kyla folded her arms across the table and lowered her head. This was too much to take in all at once.

"Ladies, I have to run, but look, why don't you guys come to dinner tomorrow? We haven't had a Sunday meal together in a long time. I know that would make Mama and Daddy happy."

"Sounds great, Gavin." Tracee arched her brows at Kyla for confirmation.

"Yeah, that sounds like a good idea. Tracee will bring dessert and we'll talk."

After Gavin hung up, a cloak of silence covered the room while Kyla cursed herself for being so self-absorbed. For the last couple of years, everything was about her and her damned PhD candidacy. Her parents lived less than an hour away, but her contact had been reduced to brief holiday visits and the occasional Sunday calls.

Tracee held the wine bottle over Kyla's glass. "Want some more?"

Kyla shook her head. "What are we going to do? We can't let them lose the place."

Tracee poured herself another glass of wine, then set the bottle down. "I don't know."

Kyla pushed the plate of brownies away. The last thing she needed to do was drown her sorrows in sugar and alcohol. She placed her elbows on the table and laced her fingers together, resting her chin on her fingers. "Tracee, we work together every day—how come you didn't tell me any of this?"

"We didn't want to worry you. With school and your program, we know you have a lot on your plate. I mean, I just found out recently. Remember when Gavin dropped by and you were headed to UK for that World Hunger Day event?"

Kyla lowered her hands. "Yeah. I thought it was strange that he came by when he usually doesn't."

"That's the day I found out. We did a little brainstorming, and he even asked if I could take out a loan. But neither you nor I are in a position to take out the kind of loan they need."

After a beat, Tracee added, "Kyla, I know you can't see this, but Miles's offer could be a godsend."

"What? Are you kidding me? Think about it Tracee—he claims he came to the B and B to learn about my program, but for what? He's not an organic farmer, he's a charmer, and he used his charm to make us feel comfortable about selling to him."

"Kyla, do you honestly believe that Miles knew that the property, which is in Mom's maiden name, belonged to your parents before he spent a week getting to know you? Then he turned around a few weeks later and flew you to Chicago so you would fall in love with him, all so he could get the land? I mean, do you honestly believe that?"

Kyla shrugged, a little unsure of herself now. "I know it sounds like a long shot, but he could have done that… couldn't he?"

Tracee tilted her head, looking skeptical. "I don't think so. You know, I'm with Gavin. Maybe we should look at Miles's offer."

Kyla cocked her head to the side. "I'm not sure it's still on the table."

"Why not?"

"I sent the real estate investor away, and after Miles came by and explained everything to me, I asked him to leave, as well. I couldn't believe it."

"You kicked them out, just like Daddy, huh?"

Kyla shrugged. For years people had been telling her she was just like her father. "Tracee, I don't want Miles to be the one who saves our family."

"But Kyla, it's business. Whatever you guys have going on personally should only help the situation, not hurt it."

Kyla leaned back in her seat. "Personally, we don't have anything going on. As fast as it started, it's over with." She sighed. "I think I just became another notch on his belt."

Chapter 20

The moment of truth finally came for Kyla when she and Tracee drove to Nicholasville for Sunday dinner with the family. After dinner, Gavin's wife, Donna, took the kids upstairs for a bath while the rest of the family gathered to discuss their financial crisis.

Her father, Ernie Coleman, sat in his broken-in easy chair, while her mother, Paula, sat on the corner of the sofa closest to him. Both of her parents were in their sixties now, and Kyla could see them moving slower than usual. Gavin initiated the conversation by asking his father if he could show the girls the papers from the man who'd offered to buy the house.

"They're in the top drawer of the dining room hutch. I haven't looked at them since he left." Ernie motioned toward the dining room.

Paula chimed in. "I told Ernie maybe we should look into this. I don't see as we have any other option."

"There you go, making it sound as if *you've* made up

our minds," Ernie complained. "That's why the girls are here, to help us decide. It's just as much their home as ours."

Paula crossed her arms. "Then you tell us what other choice we have? We've borrowed everything we can and sold whatever we could. There's nothing left to do, Ernie, but sell."

Kyla sat on the edge of her seat, holding her stomach. "Mama, you'd really consider selling the land?"

"Kyla, I know you're attached to this place, possibly more than your sister and brother, but we're going to have to face the reality of the situation. We can't afford to work this land any longer. It's taken everything we have, and we don't have any more to give," Paula said.

"I'm not attached to this place." Tracee spoke up from her chair across the room. "In fact, I'd like to see you guys in a nice ranch-style home somewhere closer to town. It's not like Kyla and I are ever going to move back in here. And I bet Gavin and Donna want their own place, instead of one that needs so much work."

Kyla looked over at her brother, who nodded in agreement before handing her the envelope that contained Miles's offer. She'd always assumed Gavin and Donna would inherit the house once their parents passed on. It never occurred to her that they might not want to stay there.

"This offer would get Mama and Daddy out of debt and I can pursue a new career," Gavin added.

Ernie looked toward the ceiling and nodded. "We may have waited too late to do something about the finances, but I always thought the Lord would work it out for us."

Gavin cleared his throat. "Did you ever think that maybe the Lord sent you Parker Edmunds? Not many people get an offer for their land right before it goes into foreclosure. And this offer leaves you guys enough money to purchase another home, something large enough for a garden out back."

Kyla's mother reached over and took her father's hand. "Ernie, I'm okay with this. As long as the family is together, does it matter where we are?"

Monday morning, Miles sat across the table from Dave, Glenda, Winston and Ralph, trying to figure out another way to help Kyla's parents while helping his business. He'd already proposed the best offer they could afford.

"What I can't understand is why they won't sell," Glenda said. "If my home were being foreclosed, I'd jump at this deal."

"It's one of the best deals I've ever seen," Dave added. "As we get closer to the foreclosure date, we might want to approach them again. If no other offers come in, they may realize it's better to sell than ruin their credit."

"Maybe we need to speak to the son," Winston added. "Do we know if the father has shared the offer with him?" He turned to Dave.

Dave shrugged. "I left a package with Mr. Coleman, but I haven't tried to reach out to the son, and personally I don't think that's a good idea. I don't even think paying them a second visit is a good idea right now. Unless we have someone in our corner, our best bet may be to wait until their backs are up against a wall."

Miles listened to his team discuss their failed efforts to purchase the land Glenda had spent so much time researching, and he felt responsible. If he'd known it was Kyla's parents' land before he invited her to Chicago, he might not have extended the invitation. The last thing he wanted was for her to think he'd given up his vow, or lied about the whole thing, just to get her cooperation. His feelings for her were real, and he hoped they would persist no matter the outcome of this deal.

"I'm going back down there," Miles said.

Everyone at the table looked at him. "Going where?" Glenda asked.

"The Coleman House B and B. I think I can talk to Kyla before it's too late."

Miles waited until the end of the week to drive down to Danville. He hadn't spoken to Kyla all week, and it was killing him. He'd booked a room under another alias, not wanting Kyla to be aware of his arrival until there was nothing she could do about it.

Tayler checked him in this time. "So, Mr. Eddie Smith, I have you down for two nights, checking out on Sunday, is that correct?" Tayler asked.

Miles detected a slight coldness in Tayler since his last visit. "That's correct."

"Well, we're certainly glad to have you." Tayler glanced around. "Does Kyla know you're staying with us?" she asked.

"No. And I'm not sure she'll be pleased, but I hope to change that before I leave."

Tayler smiled. "Let's hope so. If I can be of any assistance—" she handed over his key and receipt "—please don't hesitate to ask. Things are kind of slow this morning, so Kyla's helping with a few deliveries. She should be back before long."

He looked down at the old-fashioned metal key in his hand. "Thanks."

They'd put him in a different room this time, and he made himself comfortable. This visit wasn't about the land in Nicholasville, and it wasn't about his genetically modified seeds—this visit was all about him and Kyla.

Miles stood on the front porch of the B and B, enjoying the warm breeze. He inhaled the fresh air and smiled at two women sitting in rockers, knitting and talking. Aside from him, they were the only guests at the B and B this weekend. Without a full house, maybe he'd have more time with Kyla. A few seconds later, she pulled up and slowed before driving around to the back of the house. He was positive she'd spotted him.

He walked around back to catch up with her before she could run inside to avoid him.

All four guest bicycles were on their racks next to the staff parking spaces. He gripped one by the handlebars, and it brought back memories of the first time he'd kissed Kyla.

She exited the car wearing dark shades, in her khakis and polo shirt with her hair in her usual ponytail. Only she could make their standard uniform look so good. She closed the door and stood there, staring at him.

"Want to go for a ride?" he asked, still holding the bike's handlebars.

She held up her elbow and shook her head. "I'm still healing from the last one."

He took another deep breath and walked closer to her. She met him halfway. He needed to see her eyes to know if she was mad at him or not, but those damn glasses hid her emotions.

"What do you want, Miles?" she asked in a harsh tone.

Okay, so she was still pissed at him. "I was hoping we could talk."

She crossed her arms. "We don't have anything to talk about."

"Yes, we do. I'm afraid you've misunderstood my intentions."

"Let's see if I've got this right." She removed her shades and tilted her head. "You intended to purchase my family's farm to produce genetically modified seeds from corn, among other things, that you'll ship overseas to third-world countries while you line your pockets."

"You think my desire to feed the hungry is just a bunch of bullshit so I can get rich?"

She glanced down at her feet before giving her head a slight shake. She was trying to look cold, but the warmth in her eyes gave her away. "Maybe not intentionally, but that'll be the outcome." When she looked up at him, her mouth softened a bit.

"Kyla, with everything I've done to show you who I am, you should know better than that. But I didn't come down here to argue with you. I want to talk about us."

She lowered her arms and walked around him. "There is no us."

He grabbed her as she passed. "Kyla, come on, you aren't going to let this deal ruin what developed between us, are you?"

She stopped and looked down at his hand. He removed it. "Nothing happened between us. We just got caught up over the excitement of it all."

All the warmth was gone from her eyes, but still he didn't believe a word coming out of her mouth. He'd broken a year-long vow for this woman, and he didn't do that for nothing. "That's all it was, huh? A little weekend excitement?"

"Miles, come on, you don't really care about that. What you want is for me to help you get that land. Stop pretending you're the least bit interested in me. You played me. This country girl fell for it, but this is where it ends." With her chin held high, she turned and walked away.

He ran a hand down his face in frustration. She'd just stabbed him in the chest while he stood there looking around, contemplating his next move. He wasn't used to this type of behavior from any woman. Then again, he hadn't cared enough for any woman to do the things he was doing for Kyla. He hadn't chased a woman in so long, he couldn't even remember how. But he hoped it was like riding a bike, because he'd checked back in for another ride.

Chapter 21

Friday, Rollin elicited everyone's help for the haul of the day. It was time for the Whole Foods harvest, and they were slated to pick three hundred pounds of tomatoes over the weekend. Ben, Sean, Rollin and two other employees were hard at work in the greenhouse already. After they provided the B and B guests with a few simple instructions, they jumped in. Kyla had picked a large basketful of tomatoes, and when she turned around Miles was right there to take it from her.

"Let me help you with that." He reached out for the basket, but she pulled back.

She didn't want him there, and she definitely didn't want his help. "I can handle this. Shouldn't you be collecting your own basket?"

He motioned to a large full basket a few feet behind him. "I've already filled one, so let me dump this for you. I'm sure you're ready to start another one, aren't you?" he asked.

She gave in, not wanting to create a fuss in front of everyone. She was surprised he'd worked faster than she had. After he deposited her tomatoes, he returned with an empty basket.

"Here you go. Let's get to picking—we've got a lot of tomatoes to get out," he said before settling in and working alongside her.

She eyed him suspiciously, not sure what he was trying to prove. And why did he have to come stand right next to her?

Kyla tried to keep her eyes on the tomato vines in front of her, but Miles standing next to her in a pair of green cargo shorts and a plaid shirt with the sleeves rolled up was hard to ignore. He'd turned his baseball cap backward and was working harder than she'd ever seen him do on past visits. She could still feel his firm thighs and his arms wrapped around her body from when she'd sat in his lap.

"So, what's in store after the tomatoes?" he asked.

"We're picking peas. Then the community center is bringing some kids out for a field trip."

He nodded and kept plucking tomatoes, placing them in his basket. "We didn't harvest peas the last time I was here," he said.

"I don't remember what you did when you were here before," she said.

"I do. I remember everything we did."

Kyla stopped and placed her hands on her hips. "Are you going to follow me around all day and," she lowered her voice, "make me reminisce about your first stay?"

"Why not? Every time I see you, I reminisce about your visit to Chicago."

"That's not fair," she said, and returned to picking tomatoes before someone noticed they were bickering.

Miles stopped working. "Can we go someplace and talk?"

She looked around him at the group of people pretending not to hear them. Had he forgotten where they were? She shook her head. "No, right here is as good as anywhere. We have tomatoes to pick." They were still within earshot of the group, so she knew he wasn't going to say anything crazy.

He crossed his arms and nodded. "Okay, I just wanted to say I haven't been able to stop thinking about the night we made love."

She dropped her tomatoes and grabbed him by the arm, pulling him out of the greenhouse. "What are you trying to do? Somebody's going to hear you."

He looked around, shaking his head. "I don't care if they heard me or not. Did *you* hear me?"

"How could I not? Miles," she confessed before crossing her arms. "I don't know why you checked in here. I don't know what you expected from me. I made myself perfectly clear when you left last Saturday. You've already given it your best shot."

His whole face tightened up, and he slowly backed away. "Okay, so you want to play hardball." He turned around and headed back into the greenhouse.

She lowered her arms and whispered after him. "No. I don't want to play any kind of ball." The only reason she didn't just come out and ask him to leave was because she knew her parents were considering accepting his offer, and she really didn't want to do anything to make him take it back. But she didn't know if she could handle having him underfoot all over again, and this time under different circumstances.

After they returned to the farm and everyone vacated the truck, Miles held his hand out to help Kyla down.

"Thank you, but I can get off the truck myself. I've been doing it for years now."

"I know you can. But I'm offering you something you're not used to taking—a helping hand."

She looked down into his gentle eyes and saw nothing but sincerity. She gripped his hand and jumped down from the truck. "Thank you."

"You're welcome. Now, that wasn't so bad, was it?"

He held onto her hand like he didn't want to let go. A rush of adrenaline ran through her body, and she remembered what it felt like to be swept up into his arms and carried to his bed.

"Excuse me, Kyla, but Mrs. Tayler asked me to find you. She's leaving now and ready for you in the barn." Ben's eyes went from Kyla's and Miles's faces down to their hands. She snatched hers away from Miles.

"Okay, tell her I'll be right there."

Ben took two steps back, then spun around before taking off. Kyla could see the questions in his eyes. He was going to bug her all afternoon, so she quickly said, "I have to go cover the U-pick store. And Miles, I'd appreciate it if you *didn't* come along." She didn't give him time to respond before she turned and walked away. As much as she didn't want it to, being around him gave her wild thoughts. When he smiled over his shoulder at her, or touched her, she remembered the explosive love they'd made that first night together.

He was playing the role of concerned lover too well. Everything felt real to her body, but her mind knew better. He was an actor playing a role to get a part.

Tayler had extended the U-pick store hours this afternoon to allow local garden clubs to come out. The van arrived, and business in the barn exploded. Kyla had Ben, Sean and Kevin helping her, since Rollin and Tayler left to attend a meeting at the local Chamber of Commerce.

For a brief moment, Kyla had been able to get Miles off her brain. That is, until she spotted him carrying a bushel of green beans out to a customer's car. She met him at the door when he came back in.

"Miles, what are you doing?" she asked. "You don't work here."

"This is a working farm, though, right?" he asked with a wink.

She clenched her jaws. "It is, but guests are given work assignments. They don't just walk in and start working like they're on the payroll."

"Then why don't you give me an assignment?" he asked.

Ben walked past with a box full of small bags.

"Whatcha got there, Ben?" Miles asked.

"Fresh chocolate chip cookies from Ms. Tracee. She said to put them with the brownies. There's another box in the kitchen if you wanna help," Ben said, giving Kyla a raised-brow look.

Miles grinned at Ben and then Kyla. "Looks like I've got an assignment. I'll be right back," he said, walking backward. "You know, I love your sister's chocolate chip cookies. Maybe I can talk her out of a few."

Kyla crossed her arms and watched Miles's broad back as he walked toward the house. So now he was going to try to charm Tracee some more. If he thought all this work was going to impress her, he was wrong. He was going to wear himself out for nothing.

Several minutes later, Kevin pulled up with the last truckload of happy customers for the day, eager to weigh their haul. Kyla was happy he came in and helped, which allowed her time to run to the back cabinet for more bags. She pulled out a large bundle that needed to be cut open.

"Want me to get those for you?"

She jumped and a hand flew to her chest when Miles

appeared out of nowhere. "Oh, God, you scared me. Don't sneak up on me like that." Because of the amount of time it had taken him to get back, she was sure Tracee had served him cookies.

He held the cabinet door open. "How many of those do you need?" he asked, as he reached down and snapped the plastic strap with one hand.

He was turning into her shadow again. "I don't know, uh…about fifty. That way, Tayler won't need any tomorrow."

He counted out fifty bags and handed them over. She tried to take them, but he wouldn't let go. She tilted her head and pressed her lips together. The look in his eyes was serious as he studied her face, as if he were counting her freckles. She tugged on the bags again, but he held them tight.

"You know what you're doing to me, right?" he asked. He bit the side of his bottom lip and grinned at her.

"Miles, I'm not doing anything to you. You won't admit that it's not actually *me* you want."

"You know that's not true. I don't want anybody but you. I want you lying next to me all night again. And don't tell me my feelings are one-sided."

This was getting ridiculous. "Okay, I fell for you, and I did something I regret, but you're acting like we were more than we actually were."

"Do you really regret it?" he asked, letting go of the bags. A pained expression passed over his face, and she could see the hurt in his eyes. If there was anything she truly regretted, it was what she'd just said.

He shook his head. "I didn't break my vow for the wrong woman. I know I didn't."

Kyla held the bags close to her chest and remembered the vow he'd made with God. To remain celibate until he found a woman he wanted to spend the rest of his life with. She lowered her head as she struggled with what her heart wanted and what her head told her was true. When she looked up, Miles was gone.

Chapter 22

Instead of Kyla's usual Saturday workshop, the farm played host to twelve energetic kids and two chaperones on a field trip from the local community center. Their chaperones tried to keep them in line, but the children gave everybody a run for their money, especially Miles.

Kyla had set up several educational stations around the farm, with interactive activities at each one. Miles fell back into his teacher's assistant role, helping her out. The only problem was that she didn't want his help.

"Where do you want these?" Miles asked as he walked into the barn with a long folding table in each hand.

Due to the scorching heat, Kyla had asked Ben—not Miles—to set the last activity up in the barn behind the house. "You can set them in the middle of the floor. That's the best place to catch a breeze."

He set both tables up himself while she walked over to the counter where all the pots sat. She figured if she ignored Miles, he'd go away.

She'd figured wrong.

"Ben said the chairs were already in here somewhere," Miles said as he looked around the barn.

Kyla stopped counting seeds, a little peeved now that Ben hadn't taken care of this already. "They're stacked back there." She pointed to a corner of the barn. "Where's Ben?" she asked.

"I sent him to help Sean with something," Miles replied as he walked over to grab a few chairs.

Kyla folded her arms across her chest and cocked her head to the side. Who did he think he was? "Why did you do that?"

"Because this is the only way I can spend time with you," he said as he placed two chairs at the table and then walked toward her.

Kyla shook her head and took a step back. *Please don't come over here, and don't touch me.* She didn't want to admit it, but she was still weak for Miles. That was one of the reasons she didn't want him there. "Miles, those kids are going to come running up the path any minute now, and I'd like their seats to be waiting for them."

He closed the distance between them. Kyla couldn't look up into his eyes. Her heart beat so loud, it rang in her ears. The hairs on her arms stood up, and his magnetic energy pulled her in. She swallowed and opened her mouth to breathe.

"Don't do this to us," he whispered in her ear.

She closed her eyes as his warm breath bathed her neck and she ached for him to kiss her there. Her body trembled as a stampede of little voices sounded in the barn. She immediately looked up, placing her fingers over her lips before moving her hand down to her chest. Miles had walked over to grab more chairs for the little people gathering around the tables. Kyla took a deep breath and pulled herself together.

Once everyone was seated, she explained that, while they learned about seeds and soils, they were going to plant pea seeds to take home. Under Miles's watchful eyes, she managed to successfully complete the activity with all the children writing their names on their pots. Between smiles and playing with the kids, Miles had made every effort to let her know he wasn't going to leave her alone.

The end of the field trip was celebrated with a game of croquet. While Kyla and Miles were helping the kids plant peas, Ben and Sean had been setting up the game. In order for everyone to play, Kyla amended the rules a bit, and everyone paired up on teams. She had one team and Miles had another. The kids were having the time of their lives trying to hit the balls through the hoops, and so was Kyla, until Miles issued her a challenge.

"I bet we can beat you to the stake," Miles proclaimed, as he and his little buddy Kenny stood next to Kyla and her new friend Abby.

Kyla shook her head. "I doubt it. I've been playing croquet all my life. I'm going to teach her how to win." She smiled down at Abby with little pink ribbons in her hair.

Miles grinned. "Well, I haven't played since college, but it's like riding a bike. I still remember a few tricks I can teach my little buddy here." He handed Kenny the mallet and instructed him on how to hit the ball. After a loud crack, the ball sailed through the first two hoops.

Never one to back down from a challenge, Kyla instructed Abby, and the game was on. They took turns chasing the ball all over the yard while the kids tried to get the hang of a game they'd never played before. Other teams followed right behind them. At one point, both Kyla and Miles were positioned to go through the same hole.

Miles stood behind Kenny, grinning over at Kyla. "This is sudden death, you know. We hit the stake, and it's lights out for you two."

She bit her lip to keep from smiling back. "It's not over until you make it back, and we're going to make it back first." Kyla looked down at Abby and winked. "Isn't that right, little lady?"

Abby nodded and didn't wait for Kyla's instruction before grabbing the mallet and giving the ball a whack. Miles's little buddy did the same, and the adults lost control while the kids swung aimlessly as they giggled and played.

Kyla made the mistake of trying to stop Abby by running up behind her just as her mallet came back in full swing, making contact with Kyla's knee. She unsuccessfully tried to jump back but a bolt of pain shot through her body. Her mouth flew open and she held her breath to keep from screaming. She bent over at the waist and grabbed her knee with both hands, taking small panting breaths through clenched teeth as Abby looked back at her with a finger in her mouth.

"I'm sorry," she said before running off with her mallet to hit her ball again.

Kyla bit her lip and nodded. She lowered her head, still stifling a scream while massaging her knee. Something had to be broken, it hurt so bad.

"Do you need to wrap my T-shirt around your knee?" Miles asked.

She shook her head and raised a brow as she looked up at Miles to see if he was serious.

Smiling, he shrugged. "It did wonders for your arm."

She rolled her eyes, and couldn't help but chuckle. "No, I don't want your T-shirt! Can't you see I'm in agony here? I probably have a broken bone or two." She straightened up.

He looked at her. "If your knee were broken you wouldn't be standing here. But she did whack you pretty good. Let's check you out," he said, as he squatted in front of her.

Miles rolled her pants leg up and ran his hands over her knee. She winced.

He continued massaging it as she placed her hand on his shoulder to steady herself.

"Bend it for me," he instructed as he lifted her leg and slowly bent her knee back and forth.

She gripped his shoulder with one hand and flinched with every bend. The pain subsided as he caressed her kneecap while gently rubbing the back of her knee. For a moment, she closed her eyes, wanting to sit down and have him massage more than just her knee.

"How's that?" he asked.

"Better," she mumbled.

"What? I didn't hear you," he said, tilting his head as he released her knee.

"Much better," she said louder, removing her hand from his shoulder and shaking her leg out.

"As soon as the kids leave, we should put some ice on it."

Kyla turned her head in the direction of the children running around the yard with mallets while the chaperones and her interns chased them. Things had gotten out of hand. "Oh, my goodness, we have to get those mallets from them before somebody gets seriously hurt."

She hobbled over with Miles beside her, and gathered the group to close the game and end the field trip. Each child left with a small pot with their first organic vegetable planted inside.

Kyla sat on a lounger in her Aunt Rita's garden, her leg propped up on a chair and a bag of ice on her knee. After a long day, when her mood wasn't quite what it should be, this was her favorite place to sit and think. While she'd been seeing the kids off, Miles had gone into the house and had her Aunt Rita prepare an icepack for her.

Miles sat across nearby, smiling with bright, shiny eyes. "See, I'm not such a bad guy, am I?"

Kyla tried her best to keep the stupid grin off her face, but she couldn't hold it back. "Whatever."

Miles kept looking at her, arching one brow, then the other. "Is that a yes, no, maybe, or a hell no?" he asked, searching her face.

She shook her head. "I never said you were a bad guy."

Miles leaned forward, resting his forearms on his knees. "You accused me of trying to harm people while lining my pockets. And, more importantly, you accused me of using you, which is something I'd never do."

"So you really had no idea about the foreclosure when you met me?" she asked.

He shook his head vigorously. "None whatsoever."

She tilted her head and studied him. Would he sit here in her family's home and lie to her face?

Miles scooted closer to the edge of his seat. "Kyla, you were upset with me, and understandably so. But as I've said, I had no way of knowing you weren't aware of the situation. If I'd known, I never would have asked David to come talk to you."

"I wish you hadn't. It was embarrassing."

He lowered his head. "I know, and I'm deeply sorry." Then he lifted his head and gazed into her eyes. "I'll understand if your family doesn't want to accept my offer. But the way I feel about you has nothing to do with your parents' property. Whether they take the offer or not, I want to know that you and I will be okay. I don't want to pretend that Chicago never happened. Besides… I want my sexy vixen, Kyla, back."

Butterflies danced in Kyla's stomach as she covered her face with her hand. Chicago seemed like a lifetime ago, a time when she'd felt liberated. And that's when she'd fallen in love with Miles.

He moved from his chair to sit next to Kyla on the lounger. He reached for her wrist and slowly pulled her hand down. Tears welled up behind her eyelids. She'd wanted to believe that Chicago was a real experience for the both of them.

"You're far more important to me than this deal. You and I have a future together. We're going to change the world."

Kyla wiped at the tears rolling down her cheeks. "We're good. Miles I'm sorry for all the accusations I threw at you. And you're right, we're going to do some amazing things together."

She blinked back tears as a slow, sexy smile covered his face. She drew a deep breath through her nose and quietly exhaled. Miles leaned over and placed a hand behind her neck, bringing their faces closer before he kissed her, reminding her of everything she'd dreamed of with this man. The icepack fell from her knee to the ground as every nerve ending in her body stirred.

He wrapped his other arm around her shoulders, and she wanted to scream out to the world that she wasn't just another notch on Miles Daniel Parker's belt.

Epilogue

Two months later

Kyla had traded her standard uniform for a casual yellow-and-white sundress, perfect for a casual potluck. The Coleman House's U-pick store had been transformed for the big end-of-summer potluck. Neighbors from up and down the road came to share produce from their farms. Everything from vegetable dishes, summer salads, watermelons, fruit desserts and grilled chicken dishes were available on two long tables.

Lights were strung around the barn, and Rollin's collection of old-school music played through the speakers.

"Look at them," Tracee said as she walked up next to Kyla. "I need to grab my phone and take a picture."

Kyla stood alongside Tracee and observed her parents looking happier than she'd seen them look in a long time. A week after accepting the offer from Parker Edmunds, they'd found a nice little home with all the modern conveniences her mother longed for and enough room out back for her father to start a small garden.

Instead of Miles producing genetically modified produce on her family's land, he'd taken a step into the future by investing in her friend Rory's natural postharvest produce protection. The investment would allow them to start production.

"You know what I hate about potlucks?" Corra asked as she joined them.

"I know. The cleanup afterwards," Kyla said.

"Bingo. You think any of these folks will volunteer to stick around and help us?"

Kyla looked at Tracee, who was shaking her head.

"Well, do you know what I *do* like about our potlucks?" Kyla asked.

"All the different foods?" Corra guessed.

"No. The fellowship. I mean, what better way to celebrate the end of the summer's harvest than with all of this wonderful socializing. Look over there at the other end of the table—our guests are mingling with our neighbors. Everybody's sampling all this good food."

"And getting drunk," Tracee added.

Corra laughed. "They're only giving out small wine samples. It's not enough to get anybody drunk."

"Girl, that homemade stuff is potent. It goes straight to your head. Trust me, I know," Tracee stated.

"But that's what I love about these get-togethers. You might not have known there was a winery in the community, or a goat farm, if we didn't have these little gatherings. I love it," Kyla said.

"Oh, don't get me wrong. When Tayler suggested we start this, I was right there with her," Corra said. "Every month somebody shows up who wasn't here last month. Like Uncle Ernie. I haven't seen him in over a month."

Kyla glanced back at the table, where her parents were

joined by her Uncle Wallace and Aunt Rita. "I know. Daddy never gets down here. Don't they look so peaceful? They're all having such a good time."

"I'm going to get my phone. This is a picture moment I can't pass up," Tracee said as she took off for the house.

"I'd better go find Chris and make sure he eats something before he grabs Rollin and they start pitching horseshoes. You know once that starts they'll be playing until it gets dark."

While Corra went to look for her husband and Tracee her phone, Kyla joined her family. Every time a car came up the driveway she turned around, looking for a black SUV.

Finally, Gavin came over and sat next to her. "Did you hear the news?"

Kyla shook her head. "No, what?"

A few weeks after selling the farm, Gavin had landed a position with LSC Communications, a global leader in traditional and digital print services. He also had plans to go back to school. He and his family were staying with Donna's parents while looking for a home.

"We found a house," he said, beaming.

"Gavin, that's great! Where is it?" Kyla asked.

"Smile, you two."

When Kyla looked up, Tracee started snapping pictures.

"Well, the cavalry has arrived," Tracee said, lowering the phone and looking beyond them.

Kyla turned around to see Miles in his dark shades, along with Glenda and Brandon, coming across the grass. Her stomach still quivered at the sight of him. In the last two months, their relationship had blossomed into something she'd been looking for her whole life. She'd ended her summer stay at the B and B, and moved back to Lexington, closer to school and Miles.

He stopped to shake hands with Kevin before proceeding toward the barn. She watched as recognition slowly grew on some of their neighbors' faces. She no longer cared about keeping their relationship private. She wanted the world to know that Miles Parker was hers. She stood up. "I'll be right back," she said before walking out to meet him.

Miles greeted her with a hug and a kiss on the forehead. "Hail, hail, the gang's all here."

"I see you brought reinforcements," she said.

"The more the merrier. You did say this was a party."

After he released her, she said hello to Brandon and reached out to hug Glenda. "I'm so glad you could make it."

"As much as Miles talks about this place, I wouldn't have missed it." Glenda hugged Kyla back. "And thank you for inviting us."

Kyla shook her head. "Everybody's welcome."

"Where's your father?" Miles asked, looking around.

She gestured to her parents sitting at a table just inside the barn. Then she turned back to Miles. "I don't know how to thank you." Tracee had been right; Miles had been a godsend for her family and for her.

He reached out and stroked her cheek. "No. Thank you."

They walked inside, where Miles exchanged greetings with everyone at the table.

Kyla's father, although happy about his new house, was still a little testy about having to sell the property in the first place. She stood back as Miles walked over to him.

"Mr. Coleman, it's nice to see you again, sir," Miles said as he reached his hand out.

Ernie Coleman stood and shook Miles's hand. "Mr. Parker, I'm surprised to see you here, but yes, it's a pleasure."

"Please, call me Miles." He took a deep breath. "Sir, if you have a moment, may I speak with you alone?"

Kyla held her breath as her father and her man walked out of the barn.

"What's going on?" Tracee asked as she walked up to Kyla.

Kyla turned to her sister with wide eyes. "He loves me, Tracee."

Miles asked Ernie Coleman to walk down to the gazebo with him, where he pointed out where Kyla held her workshops. He was nervous and stalling, he knew.

Ernie crossed his arms as he stood eye to eye with Miles. "So, what's this I hear? First you came after my land...and now you want my daughter?"

Miles took a deep breath and smiled at the man he hoped one day would be his father-in-law. "Yes, sir. You might say I'm an old-fashioned kind of guy, but I wanted to speak to you and let you know how much your daughter means to me. Kyla is the woman I've been looking for all my life. We share the same passions in life, and together I know we can change the world."

Ernie tilted his head and gave Miles his best poker face.

"I wanted to let you know how much I love her, and respect her. She's the most beautiful, intelligent and loving woman a man could ever ask for." Miles cleared his throat. "And with your blessing, I'd like to ask her to marry me." The rolling feeling in Miles's stomach made him nauseated. He couldn't move as he waited for Ernie Coleman to say something, anything. The man took so long to respond, beads of sweat formed on Miles's upper lip and forehead.

"Does she want to marry you?" Ernie finally asked.

"Yes, sir. We've had numerous discussions about it. I know we haven't been together long, and we're not getting married tomorrow, but I don't need to wait any longer. I know she's the woman for me."

"What about her PhD?" Kyla's father asked.

Miles nodded. "I will fully support her in anything she wants to do. We've even discussed expanding her program after she receives her degree. I want to invest in her vision."

Ernie smiled, and held out his hand. "You have my blessing. And thank you for asking."

Miles exhaled. "Sir, there's one more thing."

When Miles and her father walked back into the barn several minutes later, Kyla was talking with Glenda and Brandon. She caught Miles's eye and the corner of his lip turned up into a smile. She loved him for what he'd just done. She'd been on pins and needles, but he was confident asking her father's permission was something he had to do. Miles walked over to her while her father joined her mother.

"Were you scared?" she asked.

Miles shook his head. "Nervous maybe, but not scared."

Her father rapped his hand against the table to get everyone's attention. Kyla turned around as Miles stood behind her and put his arm around her shoulders.

"Could I get everyone's attention please? Somebody grab my other daughter over there, talking her head off. I need everyone's attention."

Kyla looked back at Miles with narrowed eyes. "What is he doing?"

Miles shrugged. "I don't know."

Rollin and Tayler walked over to the table, along with a few neighbors. Corra, Gavin, and her Aunt Rita and Uncle Wallace were already at the table. Kyla whispered to Miles, "Hail, hail, the gang's all here."

"Ladies and gentlemen, first I'd like to thank my nephew Rollin for hosting this end-of-harvest gathering. All this good food and fellowship, it's wonderful."

The group clapped, and Rollin nodded.

"Well, that's all I've got to say, but this young man

here has something to say." Ernie pointed toward Miles and sat down.

A knot formed in Kyla's neck when Miles turned her around. She couldn't swallow. What was he doing? Glenda had moved in close to them and was wiping her eyes.

"Kyla, you know you're the woman I've spent thirty-two years looking for. I love you with all my heart. I love your intelligence, your beauty, your laser-sharp attitude." The crowd laughed at that last one. "But most of all, I love your passion for helping others, for doing what you do every day to make the world a better place."

He took a step back, reached into his pants pocket and pulled out a ring. Kyla covered her mouth with her hand. He reached out for her other hand and dropped down on one knee. The crowd gasped, and she wanted to faint. Everyone was just as shocked as she was.

"Ms. Kyla Coleman, you've already made me the luckiest guy in the world just by giving me your time. But—" he slid the ring on her finger "—will you make me the happiest man in the world? Will you marry me?"

Kyla screamed so loud that everyone on the farm heard her. "YES!"

* * * * *

COMING NEXT MONTH
Available March 20, 2018

#565 STILL LOVING YOU
The Grays of Los Angeles • **by Sheryl Lister**

Malcolm Gray is Lauren Emerson's biggest regret. Eight years ago, a lack of trust cost her a future with the star running back. Now an opportunity brings the nutrition entrepreneur home, where she hopes to declare a truce. But their first encounter unleashes explosive passion. Is this their second chance?

#566 SEDUCED IN SAN DIEGO
Millionaire Moguls • **by Reese Ryan**

There's nothing conventional about artist Jordan Jace, except his membership to the exclusive Millionaire Moguls. And when he meets marketing consultant Sasha Charles, persuading the straitlaced beauty to break some rules is an irresistible challenge. But their affair may be temporary, unless they can discover the art of love—together...

#567 ONE UNFORGETTABLE KISS
The Taylors of Temptation • **by A.C. Arthur**

All navy pilot Garrek Taylor ever wanted was to fly far from his family's past. But with his wings temporarily clipped, he's back in his hometown. His plans are sidetracked when he wins a date with unconventional house restorer Harper Presley. Will their combustible connection lead to an everlasting future?

#568 A BILLIONAIRE AFFAIR
Passion Grove • **by Niobia Bryant**

Alessandra Dalmount has been groomed to assume the joint reins of her father's empire. Now that day has arrived, forcing her to work closely with co-CEO and childhood nemesis Alek Ansah. As they battle for control of the billion-dollar conglomerate, can they turn their rivalry into an alliance of love?

Get 2 Free Books,

Plus 2 Free Gifts—

just for trying the
Reader Service!

Mr. Green stood, helped her with her chair and waved at someone. "I know you're still meeting with players, but have you had a chance to meet Malcolm Gray yet?"

The hairs stood up on the back of her neck. Before she could respond, she felt the heat and, without turning around, knew it was Malcolm.

"Congratulations, Malcolm," Mr. Green said, shaking Malcolm's hand. "Have you met Lauren Emerson? She's going to be a great asset to the team."

Malcolm stared down into Lauren's eyes. "Thanks, and yes, we've met. Hello, Lauren."

That's one way to describe it. "Hi, Malcolm." She had only seen photos of him wearing a tuxedo, and those pictures hadn't come close to capturing the raw magnetism he exuded standing next to her. She couldn't decide whether she liked him better with his locs or the close-cropped look he now sported.

"Well, my wife is going to have my head if we don't get at least one dance in, so I'll see you two later. Malcolm, can you make sure Lauren gets acquainted with everyone?"

Lauren's eyes widened. "Oh, I'll be fine. I'm sure Malcolm has some other people to see." She looked to Malcolm, expecting him to agree. To her amazement, he extended his arm.

"Shall we?"

With Mr. Green and his wife staring at her with huge smiles, she couldn't very well say what she wanted. Instead, she took his arm and let him lead her out to the dance floor. She regretted it the moment he wrapped his arm around her. Malcolm kept a respectable distance, but it didn't matter. His closeness caused an involuntary shiver to pass through her. And why did he have to smell so good? The fragrance had a perfect balance of citrus and earth that was as comforting as it was sensual. How was she going to make it through the next five minutes?

Malcolm must have sensed her nervousness. "Relax, Lauren. We've danced closer than this, so what's the problem?"

Lauren didn't need any reminders of how close they'd been in the past. "I'm fine," she mumbled.

A minute went by and Malcolm said, "Smile. You don't want everyone to think you're not enjoying my company."

She glared up at him. "You're enjoying this, aren't you?"

He grinned. "I'm holding a beautiful woman in my arms. What's not to enjoy?"

Mr. Green and his wife smiled Lauren's way, and she smiled back. As soon as they turned away, she dropped her smile. "I can't play these games with you, Malcolm," she whispered harshly.

"This is no game." Their eyes locked for a lengthy moment, then he pulled her closer and kept up the slow sway.

Don't miss STILL LOVING YOU by Sheryl Lister, available April 2018 wherever Harlequin® Kimani Romance™ books and ebooks are sold.

Want to give in to temptation with steamy tales of irresistible desire?

Check out **Harlequin® Presents®, Harlequin® Desire** and **Harlequin® Kimani™ Romance** books!

New books available every month!

***

CONNECT WITH US AT:

Harlequin.com/Community

 Facebook.com/HarlequinBooks

Twitter.com/HarlequinBooks

Instagram.com/HarlequinBooks

Pinterest.com/HarlequinBooks

ReaderService.com

**ROMANCE WHEN
YOU NEED IT**

PGENRE2017

LOVE
Harlequin
romance?

Join our Harlequin community to share your thoughts and connect with other romance readers!

Be the first to find out about promotions, news, and exclusive content!

Sign up for the Harlequin e-newsletter and download a free book from any series at
www.TryHarlequin.com

CONNECT WITH US AT:

Harlequin.com/Community

 Facebook.com/HarlequinBooks

Twitter.com/HarlequinBooks

Instagram.com/HarlequinBooks

Pinterest.com/HarlequinBooks

ReaderService.com

 **HARLEQUIN**®

**ROMANCE WHEN
YOU NEED IT**

HSOCIAL2017

Reward the book lover in you!

Earn points from all your Harlequin book purchases from wherever you shop.

Turn your points into *FREE BOOKS* of your choice
OR
EXCLUSIVE GIFTS from your favorite authors or series.

Join for FREE today at
www.HarlequinMyRewards.com.

Harlequin My Rewards is a free program (no fees) without any commitments or obligations.

MYR17